"Your mouth is just like velvet, Toni."

Jay bent to kiss her lips, and suddenly the floodgates of memory opened and Toni's senses were swamped with the familiar ignition of passion between them.

Then fear took the upper hand. Fear that she would once again be drawn into the steel web of his attraction, that she would once again take on the role of neglected wife while Jay pursued his insatiable business interests.

"It's no use, Jay," she said fiercely, pulling herself from his arms. "You'd drop me again if some crisis came up in one of your business concerns."

"If I did," he replied smoothly, "it would only be because I was safeguarding our future."

"*Your* future," she corrected him dully. "Mine lies in another direction now."

Other titles by

ELIZABETH GRAHAM

IN HARLEQUIN ROMANCES

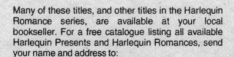

Many of these titles, and other titles in the Harlequin
Romance series, are available at your local
bookseller. For a free catalogue listing all available
Harlequin Presents and Harlequin Romances, send
your name and address to:

HARLEQUIN READER SERVICE,
M.P.O. Box 707,
Niagara Falls, N.Y. 14302
Canadian address:
Stratford, Ontario, Canada N5A 6W2

ELIZABETH GRAHAM

dangerous tide

Harlequin Books

TORONTO • LONDON • LOS ANGELES • AMSTERDAM
SYDNEY • HAMBURG • PARIS • STOCKHOLM • ATHENS • TOKYO

Harlequin Presents edition published November 1980
ISBN 0-373-10392-1

Original hardcover edition published in 1980
by Mills & Boon Limited

CHAPTER ONE

'ANY possibles coming aboard this trip?'

Toni Morelli turned from the ship's rail to smile briefly at her fellow cruise director, Carole Boyd. Her own cap of black glossy hair contrasted sharply with Carole's sophisticated blonde sweep to the back of her head and, although their scarlet uniform raincoats were identical, there was little further resemblance between them.

'A few,' Toni admitted in her slightly husky voice, her generous mouth curving into a smile of mischief. 'A couple of tall, dark and handsomes, and a sprinkling of Nordic gods.'

'Really?' Carole pressed closer to the rail, her eyes scanning the spot between arrival area and covered gangway leading up to the ship.

'Really,' Toni responded drily. 'All you have to do is throw their wives or girl-friends overboard, and they're yours for two glorious weeks.'

Grimacing, Carole turned away. 'Why is it that the best men are always taken? Why don't they ever take a cruise on their own? It's not as if I care what happens once we're back in port. No strings attached, that's me. Once bitten twice shy in the marriage game as far as I'm concerned.' Over her shoulder she tossed back: 'See you down below, sweetie. I melt in the rain!'

The steadily falling drizzle did indeed cast a pall

over the embarkation area, but Toni disregarded
the drops that made her dark hair glisten with a
myriad lights and turned her attention back to the
diminishing trickle of passengers hurrying towards
the covered gangway.

It was the same every trip. She would take her
place at this vantage point scanning the new arrivals, watching for yet dreading the recognition of
one of the winter-weary passengers eagerly antici-
pating the cruise from Los Angeles to the Mexican
sun ports of Cabo San Lucas, Mazatlan, Puerto
Vallarta, Acapulco.

Not that there was much likelihood of seeing
anyone she had known in her life with Jay Stanford.
The people they had mixed with during their brief
marriage would choose one of the sleeker, more
modern vessels to travel in than the aged but pleasantly comfortable *Aztec Queen*. The rumour was
that a prospective buyer for the old lady of the sea
would be aboard this trip. Captain Vance, who had
been in command since her teenage, neither confirmed nor denied the rumour, but his closely knit
staff had sensed his unspoken wish that everything
run smoothly on this voyage.

Toni's vivid dark eyes softened in the rainy mist
that penetrated despite the overhang of lifeboats
strung along the boat deck. Hyram Vance had been
her saviour at a time when she hadn't known where
to turn. A close friend of her Italian-American
father in Seattle, Washington, Hyram had suggested
on one of his rare leaves from the ship that she take
on the job of assistant cruise director. There was
nothing like a busy life aboard, he said, to chase

away the blues brought about by her failed marriage.

That had been two years ago, and Toni had cultivated her previously undiscovered talent of encouraging the passengers to throw off the shackles of normal shore life and enjoy the carefree games and quizzes, masquerade parties and talent nights aboard ship. At the same time, she had managed to submerge her own unhappiness, and now she thought only occasionally of her life with Jay Stanford, the year's span of her marriage to one of America's most up-and-coming industrial giants.

From occasional news reports in the papers, Jay was no longer up-and-coming. He had arrived. Interests ranging from steel to miraculously reactivated mines in the Mid-West seemingly fell into his lap, and he was now hailed as the youngest industrialist to have clawed his way to the top from relative obscurity.

Only it hadn't fallen into his lap. Toni knew that only too well. Ruthless ambition had driven him from a poverty level childhood to the pinnacle of success only because he had been willing to sacrifice other things. Things like their marriage.

The consuming love that had drawn them together initially like an obsessive magnet had burnt brightly for several months after their marriage, then gradually dimmed in the corrosion of too many late nights devoted to business, too many out-of-town trips that left Toni frustrated and lonely with too much time on her hands. The fantasy of the boss falling for and marrying one of his employees had been only too real.

Toni had been up-and-coming herself in the personnel department of Stanford Industries. Chicago had held brighter opportunities for her than her native Seattle, that opinion being confirmed when she had been hired as an assistant in the personnel department of Stanford Industries three days after arriving in the Windy City. She had moved from the Wishart Hotel for Single Girls to a small but attractively laid out apartment close to the Stanford office tower, the apartment where Jay, dwarfing it with his hard-packed bulk, had said wryly months later: 'Well, if I can't have you any other way, I guess I'll have to marry you.'

Coming from a man like Jay Stanford, that statement was unprecedented in the history of his romantic contacts. Women, even before his meteoric rise to fortune, had found his husky good looks attractive. Married or not, they had vied for his attention, and Toni was well aware on their wedding night that he was no stranger to the arts of love. She hadn't cared, knowing that from that time on he would be hers alone. She had given freely of the stored-up passion of her twenty-two years, exchanging kiss for kiss, caress for caress.

But she had been a naïve idiot in supposing that her own unsophisticated responses could satisfy the experienced senses of a man like Jay Stanford. His business was in the spiral stage then, necessitating hurried trips to New York, Milwaukee, the Mid-West. And always on those trips he had been accompanied by Gloria Powell, an assistant in the company's legal department. Tall, attractively slender, naturally blonde Gloria who made no effort to hide,

in Toni's presence, her sloe-eyed glances of possession in Jay's direction.

A possession Toni had ignored until the night she
had called Jay's hotel in Cleveland, anxious to make
up the bitter quarrel they had fought through before he left their sumptuous penthouse suite. Quar-
rels, born of frustration and loneliness, had been
becoming more and more frequent with his every
departure.

Gloria had answered his room phone despite the
lateness of the hour, her voice seductively husky
when she said: 'Jay's in the shower. Would you like
me to call him?'

That was the night Toni had packed and left Jay.
Back in the relative serenity of her parents' home
in Seattle she had waited for him to call, to come
and tell her that he couldn't live without her in the
same way that she felt a vital limb had been chopped
from her body.

But there was nothing. No call, no letter until the
notice from his lawyers had announced his intention
to seek a divorce. It was then that she had accepted
Captain Vance's offer of employment on his ship.
Jay had wanted his freedom, and she had not con-
tested his right to have it.

Now, turning away from the rail, Toni did a swift
double-take when a solitary male figure emerged
from the loading area and made a long-legged dash
for the gangway. Despite the covering of a well
pulled down hat over the face, the man's confident
set of the shoulders and quick stride could have
been Jay's. Even the bulging briefcase in his hand

added to the similarity, and Toni's hands tightened again on the rail.

Would it never end, this heartache of hopeful discovery and crushing disappointment? She hadn't seen Jay for two and a half years, yet a stranger's sudden appearance could make her heart pound, her palms grow moist.

Swinging determinedly away from the rail, Toni told herself, as she opened the heavy door into the pleasant warmth of the ship's interior, that the man had struck a chord of recognition only because she had been remembering Jay out there on the deck. With the ease of long practice, she put Jay and her past life firmly out of her mind as she stepped into the spacious entrance hall on the deck below.

Smiling, she edged through the milling passengers waiting to be directed to their cabins. It wasn't part of her job to escort newly embarked cruisers through the maze of passages to their staterooms, but she often helped out when there was a backlog and too few stewards to cope. She loved the air of excited anticipation about the entrance hall at the beginning of a cruise. Many of the passengers were sailing for the first time, and brought with them the tensions and cares of the everyday world. After two weeks on board, weeks filled with sun and relaxed gaiety, these same people would be unrecognisable.

'Anything I can do?' she murmured to Rick Warren after divesting herself of her raincoat to reveal her uniform of scarlet jacket, V-necked white silky top and matching pleated skirt.

Rick was the Purser, and took his duties very

seriously. His brows were now flexed in a familiar frown.

'Thanks, Toni. That group over there is for C Deck,' he indicated the collection of ten or twelve people beginning to move restlessly beside the elevators. 'Can you handle them?'

'Sure can,' she responded cheerfully, plunging back into the crowd from the comparative safety of the Purser's counter desk.

Pressing the elevator button, she said to the group: 'If you'd like to follow me, I'll see you to your cabins.'

'Wow!' came from one of a pair of men in their early twenties, obviously there to sample the swinging ship life promised in the brochures. 'Do you bring morning coffee to our beds, too?'

'I let the stewards have that pleasure,' she responded sweetly, ushering the group into the elevator, saying brightly as it descended swiftly to the deck four stops below: 'You'll be left on your own today to settle in and find your way around the ship. But first thing in the morning I'll be starting off the day with exercises on the Sun Deck. You'll find all the information about shipboard activities in your cabin, and please feel free to join in any of them that takes your fancy.'

'You take my fancy,' the swinging young man murmured as he followed closely on her heels along the seemingly endless passage that dipped down in the middle before rising again to the bow. 'How about us getting together on your time off?'

'Once we're under way, I have very little time off,' Toni told him crisply, thankful that his and his companion's cabin was one of the first on their route.

The entrance hall was empty of passengers on her return, and Rick's brow had relaxed its tension. Leaning with her elbows on the broad wooden counter, Toni said with a teasing smile:

'I see I'm not needed any more.'

'You'll always be needed where I'm concerned,' Rick said, his voice emotionally husky. 'You don't need to be told that.'

She didn't. At the merest drop of a hint, she knew that Rick would marry her and do everything in his power to make her happy. He was nice, clean-cut, serious—maybe too serious, she thought as she studied his fair straight hair brushed precisely back from his quietly handsome face. Jay had been serious when business dictated, but with her he had been the opposite. Their sense of humour had coincided under the most ridiculous circumstances, drawing them together in a closeness that was now hard to break when other men appeared on Toni's horizon.

Jay again! Why couldn't she forget him? she wondered furiously as she made a lighthearted rejoinder to Rick and went below to the cabin she shared with Carole on E Deck above the throb of the engines. Divorce was as final as you could get in a marriage, and she and Jay were divorced. Not even the fire that had razed her parents' home in Seattle and taken her father's life immediately, her mother's days later in hospital, could wipe out her mother's last words.

'Letter ... Jay's lawyers ... came a few days ago.' Her mother had raised her head with the last of her strength to look fiercely into Toni's eyes. 'Find a good man to ... care for you ... love you. ...'

'I will, Mamma,' Toni had choked, knowing that the letter her mother spoke of must be the final divorce papers she had waited to receive. She had done nothing to obtain copies of the legal notation of the divorce. It would be easy enough to obtain proof if the time arose when she wanted to marry again.

Now that time might be here, she pondered, throwing herself on the narrow bunk separated from Carole's by a four-drawer chest topped by a square mirror. She couldn't go on forever remembering Jay and the love they had shared once upon a time. Part of her would never forget the golden nights when passion had wiped out everything else but the need to give, to receive.... Always in the background of Toni's consciousness was the incredible changeability of Jay's eyes from the cool grey of business concerns to the warm vitality of a mutually shared love commitment.

'Hi,' Carole breezed in suddenly, looking critically at Toni's prone figure as she threw off the outer emblems of her servitude to the *Aztec Queen* company. 'Why so glum? Has our esteemed Purser thrown you over for the glamorous blonde staked out on S for Special Deck?' Wrapping a silky robe around her attractively moulded figure, Carole stepped towards the bathroom adjoining their cabin. 'As long as she keeps her well-kept talons off the dishy character I glimpsed coming aboard at the last minute, I won't have any quarrel with her. Rumour has it,' she paused with her hand on the doorknob, 'that he's the Mr Brownlea who's looking the old tub over with a view to buying her.'

'Doesn't it bother you that some stranger is aboard, spying on our every movement?'

Carole threw open the door to their small shower bathroom. 'Not if he means to make some badly needed changes around here. Like putting the entertainment staff in quarters where the shower runs hot instead of lukewarm or outright cold, and siting them where the stabilised motion of the sea, not the boneshaking throb of the engines, lulls them to sleep.'

'Dreamer,' Toni smiled at the closing bathroom door. No businessman with an eye to profits would dream of housing the staff in quarters such as Carole envisaged. Paying passengers always had the pick of the accommodation, and rightly so. But still the company lost money steadily.

That thought led to another. Would this Mr Brownlea be the kind of man to appreciate the finer qualities of the *Aztec Queen*, the ones that didn't show on a ledger balance? Some people made an annual affair of their cruise on the old ship, liking the uncrowded conditions and friendliness of the crew. Factors which returned little in a commercial sense. Jay, with his acute business acumen, would have——

Sighing, Toni rose from her bunk. If she was to join with the rest of the crew in impressing Mr Brownlea with the worthiness of the *Queen*, it would be best if she put comparisons with Jay completely out of mind.

*

'. . . and bend . . . and stretch . . . and bend . . . and—relax.'

Toni straightened a fraction before the handful of early morning exercisers and watched as they returned to a standing position, dropping their arms to their sides with relief, yet their wind-whipped faces showed a healthy colour that proved the benefit of the exercise session. It was never a chore to Toni to take the early exercise programme. Carole shone in the late evening, while preferring the early hours spent in the warmth of her bunk.

'Excuse me, miss,' the voice of Captain Vance's English steward sounded at Toni's side. 'Cap'n Vance would like to see you in his quarters.'

'*Now?*' Toni slanted sideways to the small, perky steward.

'Yes, miss. He's waiting for you in his sitting room.'

'Oh. Well, tell him I'll be along as soon as I've changed into uniform.'

'Pardon me, miss, but the captain says you're to come as you are.'

'All right, Copie, I'll be there in a couple of shakes.'

A frown worried her brow as she watched the tiny Cope disappear in the direction of the Captain's quarters. It was unusual for Captain Vance to call one of the entertainment staff to his quarters, unheard of at this early hour.

Hyram Vance, his seamed and sea-warmed complexion dearly familiar to her, motioned to the tray of coffee and doughnuts on his buffet table when she knocked and entered his wood-lined sitting room.

'Help yourself, Toni,' he said in his gruff voice. 'Sorry to drag you away from your breakfast, but it's important.'

'I guessed it must be,' Toni returned, crossing to the buffet and pouring herself a thick white mugful of dark coffee. 'Something wrong, Captain?'

'Wrong? No. Not so far anyway.' The stocky body in tropical whites moved to stand beside her at the buffet, his hand automatically reaching for the coffee pot. 'You may have heard, Toni,' he went on, waving her to a comfortable armchair, 'that we have a very important passenger on board.'

'Mr Brownlea?' she asked shrewdly.

'Yes. He—represents a company that might be interested in investing in the *Queen*.' He paused, then went on heavily: 'I don't need to tell you how important it is to the continuation of the run that he's —favourably impressed by our efficiency, by the goodwill we generate among the passengers.'

'Of course, sir. I'm sure I speak on behalf of all the crew when I say that we'll do everything we can to——'

The deep-toned voice cut across her stilted words. 'I know I can rely on the crew, Toni. It's just that— oh, hell, there's so much wrong with the old gal, I can't see that anybody would want to take her over as a paying proposition.'

Toni loyally defended the ship that was necessary to so many people apart from the crew. 'Captain, anybody can take a cruise to Mexico these days on ships that are fitted out with every luxury imaginable, and a lot of people do. But the *Aztec Queen* offers so much more in the way of atmosphere, service, real relaxation.'

Hyram Vance chuckled unexpectedly. 'You've convinced me, Toni. Now all you have to do is win over Mr Brownlea in Special Cabin 6! He wants to see you in his stateroom right away.'

'Me?'

'He means to interview each member of the crew, starting with you.' A twinkle lit the blue eyes. 'Maybe he's heard already that Boyd isn't at her best until the afternoon.'

Toni drained her coffee cup and rose lightly to her feet. 'I'd better go and change,' she said, glancing down at the white-edged scarlet of her sweat suit.

'No,' the captain said thoughtfully. 'Maybe it's best if you present yourself in working garb. That way he'll know that the entertainment staff doesn't just blossom out when the band's playing.'

Toni still wasn't sure that exercise gear was the correct dress for an initial interview when she tapped lightly on the dark panelled door of Suite 6. She would have possessed more confidence in the neat symmetry of her scarlet and white uniform dress.

A muffled male voice told her to enter, and she pushed open the door into the luxury suite consisting of king-sized bedroom and seascape living room with wide windows looking directly on to the sparkling blue of ocean and sky. From the spacious bathroom immediately to her left, she heard the vague instruction to make herself at home. The hum of an electric razor made it obvious what the suite's occupant was doing, and she fumed silently as she passed through the sleeping quarters with their tumbled king-sized bed and into the brilliant natural light of the sitting room. Taking a stance by one end of the encompassing windows, she wondered irritably why the suite's occupier had decided to start his staff interviews so early in the day. Surely it would have been better to wait until he was personally presentable.

Probably Mr Brownlea had all the arrogance of every successful business man she had known in her life with Jay. Sure of the power money have them, confident in their own invincibility.

'Sorry to have kept you waiting, Antonia.'

Toni's vision melded and froze in the blue rise of ocean beyond the windows. She must be going crazy! The faceless Mr Brownlea had assumed the voice of Jay, speaking her name in its fulness as only he had ever done.

Her head swivelled slowly round to the spot where the voice came from.

CHAPTER TWO

'IT *is*—you.'

Toni's shocked eyes took in the familiarly well-knit frame, the thickness of dark brown hair above eyes as steely grey as ever as Jay crossed the bedroom to the sitting area.

'It sounds as if you expected me.'

His voice held the same magic it had always held for her. She ran her tongue over a lower lip suddenly dry. 'I—expected Mr Brownlea.'

'Mr Brownlea was unfortunately detained. I've taken his place.'

The stunned brown of Toni's eyes met the bland grey of his. Had there ever been a Mr Brownlea? Or had Jay, for reasons of his own, booked the cruise under a fictitious name? Once the initial shock of seeing Jay again subsided a little, Toni was conscious only of a sharp pang of disappointment. Captain Vance had been pinning most of his hopes on impressing Mr Brownlea and so saving the *Aztec Queen* from the scrapyards. Jay's analytical mind would instantly weigh up the pros and cons as he did in all his business deals, and she knew which side would tip the balance in his estimation. Besides, shipping wasn't in his line.

'Why are you doing this, Jay?' she asked huskily, blinking away the sheen of moisture from her dark eyes.

For a long moment he looked calculatingly back at her, then said softly: 'Does it matter that much to you?'

'Of course it matters!' she threw back hotly. 'Captain Vance thought that Mr Brownlea might persuade his company to—buy the *Queen*.'

'As it happens, Brownlea works for me. What makes you think I won't be just as interested in buying?' Jay took a pack of cigarettes from his shirt pocket and lit one before going to perch casually on the broad window ledge, his features darkened against the light behind him so that his expression was difficult to see. He must have resumed the habit he had given up on their marriage, telling her that he had no need of any other crutch but her.

'You?' she scorned. 'You never buy into anything unless it's a red-hot moneymaker!'

'And the *Queen*'s not that?' he put with shrewd quickness, and her eyes fell away from his.

'She could be, with a few improvements.'

'A few?' he laughed mockingly. 'From what I've seen already, she needs overhauling from keel to topside, or whatever the nautical terms are.'

'But she's worth it,' Toni cried, then bit her soft underlip. 'Jay, did you really come aboard to look her over, or is this all a put-up-job?'

'I had more than one reason,' he conceded lightly, blowing smoke into the air from his tautly shaped mouth. He looked at the burning tip of his cigarette. 'Mainly, I wanted to see how my wife is doing without me.'

Toni's head reared back, the outside light falling directly on her, making a blue-black glossy band round her hair. 'I'm doing just fine, not that it's any of your business now. You divorced me, remember?'

She had never actually seen anyone freeze before, but that was what Jay did now. The only movement about him was the spiral of blue smoke arising from the cigarette he held close to his face.

Then his hand dropped to the ashtray beside him and he crushed the remainder of the cigarette into the metal.

'We've never been divorced, Toni. You're still my wife.'

There was no noise in the stateroom at all, apart from the sudden rapid pound of Toni's heart, which filled her ears and made her oblivious to everything else.

Dimly, she heard Jay's tight voice. 'Didn't you get the letter telling you I'd changed my mind? Here, sit down.'

Even through the thickness of her sweat-shirt his touch was warm as he lowered her to an armchair facing the windows, then her head was being pressed down to her knees. The action cleared her brain, and she struggled upright against the confining hand at her nape, looking disbelievingly up into Jay's tautly set face.

'That must have been the—letter Mom told me about before she—died,' she faltered. 'The one that was burned in the fire.'

'Fire? What fire?'

His eyes were suddenly on a level with hers as he knelt beside the chair.

'The house—it burned down about a year ago.'

Her voice was wooden now. 'Dad was—killed right away, but Mom was still alive when I got back to Seattle. She told me about—the letter from the lawyers. I thought——' she buried her face in her hands and finished on a muffled note: 'I thought it was the final divorce papers.'

She was gathered roughly in Jay's arms and lifted from the chair to be pressed against the hard warmth of his chest.

'Why didn't you tell me?' he groaned against her hair. 'Dammit, if I'd known——'

Toni tore herself from the comforting embrace, hating the way she had succumbed so readily to the old magic he exuded.

'Why would I let you know?' she said bitterly, going to lean against the stalwart support of the bulkhead frame. 'You weren't interested enough to come and see me—even to feed me lies about why Gloria was in your room at midnight.'

Jay spun her round so sharply that she would have lost her balance if he hadn't gripped her shoulders in a hard grasp.

'That's why you left?' he asked incredulously. 'Because of Gloria?' The line running from nose to mouth deepened perceptibly. 'If Gloria was in my room at midnight, then it was for business purposes only.'

'And I suppose you were cooling off in the shower after a heavy *business* session?' She lifted her dark arched brows sarcastically.

'Gloria never meant anything to me from long before our marriage,' he gritted between strong white teeth.

Then, like a scene from a light comedy, there was a preliminary tap on the door and Gloria Powell herself swept into the suite. Svelte in a pale coral pantsuit, the fair-haired sophisticate had reached the near end of the bedroom area before she noticed Toni held firmly between Jay's hands.

'Jay, I'm going to tell you again that this whole idea is absolutely cra—oh!' Her face went several shades of red, then settled on a patchy white. 'It's *you*!'

'It's me,' Toni confirmed flatly, pulling out of Jay's arms and flashing him a look of contempt as she moved towards the door. 'But don't let me interrupt your—business talk.'

Feeling at a distinct disadvantage in the baggy contours of her sweat-suit, Toni left the suite and strode quickly to the elevator that would take her to the nether regions where her cabin was located.

Carole was still a rounded outline under the covers.

The shock of seeing not only Jay but the woman who had broken up their marriage sent her mind into a state of suspended animation as she showered quickly and changed into her uniform, her arms a tanned dark brown against the white of her sleeveless top. Amazingly, it was still only a little after eight-thirty when she stepped into the midship dining room, where a staff table was reserved towards the rear. At lunch and dinner the table was a hub of conviviality, generated mainly by the entertainment staff of Carole and Toni, but now only one of the two nurses on board greeted Toni as she took her place at the round table.

'Hi, Tony,' Trudy Fleming said morosely over her half finished breakfast of crisp fried bacon strips, eggs and hash brown potatoes, a steady diet of which food maintained the ample contours of her white-clad figure. 'What's new with you?'

'You wouldn't believe,' Toni returned darkly, giving her order to the white-jacketed waiter who came up at that moment. 'Grapefruit, toast and coffee, please, Mario.'

The lift of his eloquent black eyebrows was purely Italian. 'On such a diet, Signorina Morelli, you will never find a man worthy of you.'

'Then I'll just have to settle for less,' Toni quipped with a lightness she was far from feeling.

Why *had* Jay decided to make this trip on the *Aztec Queen*? The question worried at her all the time she was sipping on the strong brew Mario placed at her elbow. She couldn't believe that he was seriously interested in buying the old ship. By most businessmen's standards, she was the proverbial white elephant—desirable, yet uneconomical. So Jay's motives must lean in another direction.

Herself? No, there had been plenty of time for a reconciliation if that was what he had desired. He hadn't cared enough to follow her to Seattle. He had let her go, as if it didn't matter to him any more, as if she didn't matter to him any more. The note she had left for him had given him no inkling of the jealous rage tearing at her insides each time she wondered how often he had gone straight from her arms to Gloria Powell's. In fact, the other woman had spent more hours in his company than Toni, his wife, had.

As she started on the tart juiciness of the half grapefruit Mario brought to her, Toni felt afresh the shock of knowing that she was still married to Jay, still his wife. For so long she had assumed herself to be a free woman, liberated from one marriage and legally entitled to contemplate another, that the thought still stunned her that she was by law still bound to Jay.

Laws. What did they mean when a man and a woman no longer had any viable emotional ties to bind them? Nothing at all. The legal details could be disposed of at any time.

Yet was she being truly honest with herself in denying the betraying leap of her pulses when Jay had held her in his arms up there in his stateroom? It was as if the time between had never been, for those few brief moments. Her entire being had yearned with an old longing for the feel of his lithe male body seeking the warm softness of hers, the sweet triumph of his possession——

Toni dropped her spoon with a clatter on the grapefruit dish and pushed her chair back with a convulsive movement.

'Are you all right, Toni?' Roused from her state of torpor, Trudy's anxious nurse's face loomed briefly on the periphery of her vision.

'Yes, I—I'm just not very hungry this morning, and I just remembered that I have to organise the children's swimming competition.'

With that impromptu excuse, Toni stumbled from the carpeted dining room and found herself minutes later at the Purser's desk with no clear memory of how she had got there. Marian Lester,

the colourless Assistant Purser, eyed her ambiva-
lently from behind the desk. It was no secret aboard
ship that Marian worshipped the ground Rick Warren walked on, and that Rick appreciated her
mainly for her quality of calm efficiency in dealing
with irate passengers and minor crises which inevitably arose on a day to day basis.

Toni had often thought that Marian could be
much more attractive in her appearance if someone
with a little know-how took her in hand. As it was,
with her off-blonde hair drawn back into an unin-
spiring bun at the back of her head, her face
unadorned by cosmetics, she was the picture of
stark efficiency in her white uniform with its
epaulettes of navy and gold on her shoulders denoting her rank on board ship.

'Rick's with the Captain right now,' she told Toni.
'Can I help you with something?'

Toni eyed her blankly, then collected herself with
a supreme effort. 'Er—yes, I'd like to have a list of
all the children under twelve for the swimming
contest this afternoon. Can you find it for me?'

'I certainly hope so,' Marian returned drily, 'considering I typed it up myself.'

Her starchily dressed form moved contemptu-
ously away in the direction of the inner office where
all the internal paperwork of the ship went on.
Within minutes she had returned with a neatly
typed list of possible participants in the swimming
competition.

'Thanks a lot,' Toni was saying with abstracted
gratitude as she glanced down the list, when Rick
Warren's busy figure crossed the hall to stand
beside her familiarly.

'Well, hello, Toni,' he said with a husky awareness which obviously set Marian's teeth on edge. 'Can I help you with something?'

Toni lifted the neatly typed list of names from the counter. 'No, thanks, Marian's done the necessary.'

Rick followed her to the far side of the entrance hall. 'Can I see you tonight after dinner?'

It wasn't unusual for her to meet Rick when the evening festivities were under way to take a walk along the moon bathed deck, usually talking of the subject closest to his heart—the early landings along the North American shores of such greats as Captain Cook, Valdez, Vancouver. Tonight, however, she knew that there would be other things on her mind.

Things like Jay's disturbing presence on the luxury deck above. And Gloria's....

'Let's play it by ear tonight, Rick,' she answered briskly, already stepping towards the elevator. 'I have an idea that this cruise is going to be different from most.'

For her it was. The moment she stepped into the flower-bedecked dining room she was conscious of an added tension in her own sinews, an atmosphere that extended to her awareness of the happily dining people on either side as she made her way to the cruise staff table at the rear.

It seemed inevitable that, once she had taken her place at the far end of the large round table, her eyes should lift to glance round the dining room and meet the steely grey of Jay's at the Captain's table.

After a fraught moment, her eyes flickered to the woman set possessively at his right hand. Gloria. As brittly beautiful as ever in a dress of shimmering blue that left her shoulders bare apart from shoe-string straps encircling her elegantly long neck.

The filmy black of her own dress, one of the six she interchanged on cruise evenings, seemed tawdry and dull compared to the iridescent glitter of Gloria's. But what did that matter? Jay had made his choice long ago. Toni was no longer in the run-ning for his romantic attention.

Dancing took place after the leisurely dinner in the beautifully decorated forward lounge. Apart from the younger set, who found their metier in the discotheque far above on the Sun Deck, most of the passengers passed at least an hour or so in the con-viviality of the Bronze Room, where more sedate dancing took place in between the top quality en-tertainment provided by fairly well known stars of stage and screen. True, many of the performers were better known for their television commercials than for their current acting prowess on the screen, but they were familiar figures and as such received their due share of adulation from the captive audience.

Toni wasn't needed on this particular evening, when Merla Merconi sang the nostalgic songs of twenty years before to an entranced audience, most of whom remembered her early light romance films of the fifties.

So when Rick bent to her ear and said: 'Need a breath of air?' she got up gladly from her seat at the rear of the ballroom and allowed him to lead her to the breeze-filled deck adjoining the lounge.

'What's your table like this trip?' Toni asked as their steps merged on the sun-bleached boards of the deck.

'As usual,' Rick grumbled dourly. As the Captain's table was the dominating factor in the Acapulco Room, so the Purser's was the focal point of the Mazatlan Room. Having the two dining rooms made it possible for everyone aboard to dine at one sitting. 'Two hopeful spinster ladies, and two long-married couples.'

'At least you won't get into any trouble this time around,' teased Toni, referring to the two unattractive daughters of an obsessively fanatical religious minister and his wife who had shared his table on the last trip. The daughters had combined in their pursuit to make Rick's life unbearable.

'I wouldn't get into any trouble at all if I could say I have a wife in port,' Rick said seriously, drawing her to a halt by the rail and retaining a hold on her arm. 'You know I'm crazy about you, Toni.'

'Oh, Rick, I——' Toni stared helplessly up into the blue eyes, darkened now by the night that enfolded them astern. What could she say to him? That her ex-husband—no, her *husband*—was aboard and that he exuded as much attraction for her now as he had when she was a naïve girl of twenty working in his office?

No, she'd be damned if she let Jay Stanford interfere in her life now. He had created enough havoc in the past.

'Show me, Rick,' she pressed herself urgently to his square-set body, 'show me how crazy you are about me.'

Rick responded as she had known he would, pulling her into his arms and covering her mouth with the softness of his. A softness that never hardened to passion as Jay's had when they made love.

Drat Jay! Would she never forget the treacherous tide of passion his most casual kiss could provoke?

As she broke from Rick's hold, she fancied she saw a shadowed movement upward on the companion-way close to them. Mentally shrugging, she smoothed the dark cap of her hair. What did it matter if a passenger had witnessed a kiss between crew members? Most of them were too absorbed in their own affairs to be bothered by anyone else's.

'You're still crazy about that husband of yours,' Rick accused baldly.

'My——?' Toni swung round bewilderedly, the velvet glaze of her eyes staring directly into Rick's.

'You can't let yourself go with any other man, can you, Toni?' he asked savagely. 'He must have been some guy!'

'He was,' said Toni, suddenly calm as she turned away to clasp the rail and stare far out to the black-ened sea. 'It just happened he wasn't my kind of guy.'

She felt Rick's hand on her bare shoulder and re-pressed a sudden shiver.

'Who *is* your kind of guy, Toni? Somebody like me?' Rick twisted her arm painfully so that she faced him.

'I don't know, Rick,' she said, anguished. 'Please —leave me alone for now.'

'My pleasure,' he told her with frightening cold-ness, and stalked away from her.

She watched his stocky figure disappear round the brilliantly lit bow, then bent her head to the foam-ing sea spray far below her, tossed up from the in-cisive slice of the *Queen*'s bow as she ploughed her steady course to Cabo San Lucas. When the passengers woke with the morning sun, they would be anchored in the wide-mouthed bay encompassing the southernmost point of the Baja Peninsula. All day long, excursion boats would ply between the ship and the sun-dried settlement, the first port of call on the ship's itinerary.

Why had Jay come back to haunt her? To stir up memories that were best laid to rest? She might have found contentment, and a measure of happiness with Rick. Not the swift rushing madness of the senses she had known with Jay, but a calm and serene affection which would outlive the swift burning fires of passion.

Jay had been aboard for little more than twenty-four hours, yet he had effectively destroyed the tenuous skeins of a relationship that might have been good.

'I hate him,' she murmured aloud, but the sea flowed uncaring past, carrying her words to the oblivion of the black void the ship left in its wake.

Below, she tossed restlessly on her bunk until Carole crept into the cabin with exaggerated care and tripped over the small but sturdy table between the beds.

'It's okay, Carole,' said Toni, sitting up and reaching for her bedside lamp switch. 'I'm not asleep.'

'I'm thankful for that small mercy at least,' Carole returned wryly, rubbing her chafed shin in the subdued light, her dress of shimmering green falling back from the slender length of leg she propped up on her own bunk. 'How come you're in bed so early?'

Toni glanced at the red leather travel clock perched on the dresser beside her bed. 'Two a.m. isn't exactly early,' she observed drily.

Ignoring that, Carole hopped to the dresser and dropped her necklace and earrings on the dresser before reaching for the zipper at the back of her dress.

'I'm going to have the most marvellous time on this cruise,' she purred with a relish long familiar to Toni. 'Mike's not one of your Adonises, but he's fun to be with for two weeks, anyway.'

'Mike?'

'Mike Parrish,' Carole explained as she slid from the figure-hugging dress, letting it drop to the floor while she groped for her wispy nightdress laid out on her bunk. Almost accusingly, she turned to say tartly to Toni: 'He's divorced, and completely un-accompanied. How come you slipped up on your spying session up top?'

'Sorry,' Toni murmured, amused. 'He must have snaked his way aboard without my eagle eye notic-ing. What's he like?'

Carole paused on her way to the bathroom. 'Not bad looking,' she said consideringly, 'but no great shakes in the Mr World class. Nothing like our Mr Brownlea, of course—he's a dream, have you met him yet?' Fortunately the blonde head disappeared at that moment, so Toni was spared a reply.

She was thoughtful as the sounds of Carole's teeth cleaning issued from the small bathroom. Of her fellow cruise director she had seen little all day, and now she reflected that maybe that was all to the good. Jay evidently intended to keep up the myth about the mysterious Mr Brownlea, for reasons of his own. Could he really be interested in buying and running the *Queen*? It would be a challenge, certainly, and different from anything he had tried before. His reason for being aboard could hardly be herself.

He had brought Gloria Powell, her arch-enemy, along.

CHAPTER THREE

TONI was summoned to Special Suite 6 again the following morning, but this time she was dressed for off-duty relaxation in short white shorts and pale blue cotton top which left most of her shoulders and back bare to the sun.

Most of the passengers had gone ashore in the constantly plying cruise boats, but Toni had decided to stay on board this time. The last thing she wanted to do was run into Jay and Gloria exploring the small Mexican resort.

'This is my off-duty time,' she said crisply to a similarly light-clothed Jay who responded to her sharp rap on the suite door.

'Is a member of the crew ever off duty?' he queried with a coolness that started her blood warming to boiling point. 'In fact, I want to talk to you about just that. Come in.'

She followed him resentfully through the meticulously made up bedroom to the sitting area, acknowledging against her will that only Jay could look that good in shorts that left most of his long legs bare. The flat muscles at the back of his thighs led to leanly rounded calves, all in the best traditionally manly way. Even his feet were bare, she noted, so it wasn't likely that he was planning a trip ashore.

'Have you been to Cabo San Lucas before?' she

34

asked pointedly, glancing through the window to where the sun-drenched town embraced the azure curve of the sea.

'Not that I can recall,' he returned with a sour look in the same direction. 'And I'm sure I would recall a place with a name like that, coming after that long stretch of desert.'

'They say the fishing is fantastic here. Deep sea stuff, with wonderful trophies to take home and decorate your walls.'

His grey eyes flicked disparagingly to hers. 'You can cut the cruise director's bright chatter while you're in here. As I've said, I want to talk to you about protocol.'

'Protocol?'

Jay thrust his big hands into the pockets of his shorts, stretching the material tautly over his hips as he moved closer to the window and stared out at the tropical scene.

'Last night you were consorting with another crew member in a'—he paused and frowned—'in a way that left little to the observer's imagination.' His mouth twisted in a parody of a smile. 'The idea is to sell the *customers* on the possibilities of romance at sea, not the crew.'

Toni, gaped at him, unbelieving. What possible business was it of his that—— Stiffly, she said: 'If you're referring to the incident with Rick Warren——'

'That's exactly what I'm referring to,' he bit off irritably, swinging back to give her the full benefit of his steel grey gaze. 'You're here to perform a duty, not to promote distaste in the paying passengers.'

'*What?*'

'In future there's to be no hanky-panky with the crew, no romance on the afterdeck. For one thing,' he pronounced grimly, 'you're a married woman, and——'

'That's something I intend to remedy the minute we're back in L.A.,' Toni cut in with a voice crystal-edged with anger. 'A divorce now is just a legal technicality. You can bet your boots that the first thing I'll do is contact a lawyer!'

Jay's dark brows rose with maddening unconcern. 'I don't think you'll do that, Antonia. You're a soft-hearted girl, as I remember, and you couldn't stand to have the Captain and crew of this ship on your conscience.'

'On *my* conscience? That's a laugh! Unlike you, I don't have that much power.'

'It's possible,' he smiled, so smugly confident that Toni stared at him suspiciously. 'In fact, I'll go so far as to say that you have the fate of the ship, Captain and crew right in the palm of your capable little hand.'

'Stop talking nonsense, Jay. Why don't you come right out with your reason for coming on this cruise? I'll be darned if I can think of a valid one.'

'Can't you?' he asked softly, stepping silently over to her, his broad hand with its square, well-kept fingernails coming up to caress lightly along the line of her cheek, making her flinch away instinctively from the touch she craved yet dreaded. Jay's mouth firmed and the lines deepened beside it.

'All right, I'll tell you why I came. I found out where you were working,' he said coolly, the slight hesitation telling Toni that he had probably employed private detectives to ferret out her whereabouts, 'and I decided that enough was enough. I want you to come back to me, Toni, and be my wife again.'

'Never!' The response was purely automatic, coming as it did from the far regions of her subconscious where she had stored all the hurt pride, heartache and anguish. Shock gave way to anger, and her brown eyes blazed into the calm grey of his. 'So you've got around to using blackmail in your business tactics, have you?'

'There are elements of blackmail in all forms of business,' he shrugged, unruffled. 'Even personal relationships.'

'That's all our marriage ever meant to you, isn't it?' Toni spoke bitterly, moving away from the chilling cold of the ceiling air conditioner to the warmth nearer the windows. 'A business type relationship.'

His voice came huskily from behind her shoulder. 'I think you know that's not true. Your memory can't be that bad.'

'My memory is excellent,' the bitterness in her voice deepened. 'All those idle days and long nights when my husband was more interested in wheeling and dealing than in working at making our marriage a good one.'

She felt his hands, warm and vibrant, clasp the cool skin of her shoulders. 'I told you at the time that it wouldn't always be that way,' he said quietly. 'A couple of years, I said, and it's been just about that.' A caustic note marred his voice. 'But you couldn't wait, could you, Toni? You wanted all of me at a time when it just wasn't possible.'

'And it's possible now, is that what you're saying?' Her shoulders grew taut under his hands.

'That's what I'm saying. From now on the business will almost run itself, with just supervision from me. We'll have time for all those things you wanted to do, and have ...' his voice dropped again to huskiness, 'like a baby.'

Toni whirled on him furiously. 'Don't you dare try to bribe me with *that* promise! When I wanted, *needed* a baby to love and care for, you wouldn't agree.' She made a dismissing gesture with her hands. 'It's too late now for all this, Jay.'

'Is it?' He caught her to him, his eyes raking her startled face. They were no longer cold and steely. 'Is it, Toni?'

Desperately Toni reached for the fury that had filled her only a moment before, but it rapidly dissipated beyond retrieval when the familiar scent of his recently showered body filled her nostrils, his breath fanned her face warmly, and the rock hardness of his powerful thighs turned her own suddenly trembling flesh to yielding softness.

'No,' she breathed as his face came nearer, but even to her own dimmed hearing the sound was far from convincing. Jay ignored the weak protest and touched her full lips with the male hardness of his ... and she was lost.

It was as if his mouth held the power of an electric shock, opening the floodgates of memory and swamping her senses with the familiar ignition of passion between them. It had never needed much—

a touch, a caress, a kiss, any one of them sufficient
to light the fires of desire, which could be quenched
in only one way.

With no more thought than the instinctive raising of a flower to the sun, Toni's lips parted to permit the heady plunder of his mouth.

When Jay's head lifted some time later, it was to
murmur raggedly against the thundering pulse at
the hollow of her throat:

'You have a mouth like velvet, Antonia, and a
body made for loving.'

As if to illustrate his words, he sent his hands
under the cotton top to cup and mould the bare outlines of her well formed breasts. The touch thrust
such a searing agony of desire through her that her
breath seemed suspended, her consciousness hanging in some kind of limbo between longing and
fear.

Fear all at once took the upper hand. Fear that
she would once again be drawn into the steel web
of his attraction, that she would once again take on
the role of neglected wife while Jay pursued his own
insatiable interests.

No, she told herself fiercely as she pulled herself
from his arms and spun away from him, smoothing
the pale blue top over her swollen breasts in an instinctive gesture. She wasn't going to give him the
chance to do that to her again.

'Toni?'

'It's no use, Jay,' she said jerkily with her back to
him. 'I don't want to get into that old hassle again.'

His hand on her arm was impatient as he swung
her round to face him.

'What in hell do you mean by that? I've told you that things will be different from now on. Don't you believe me?'

Toni no longer had to school herself in indifference to his touch. The heat of passion had frozen into an ice block inside her.

'I believe you mean it right now, Jay,' she said wearily, 'but you'd drop me like yesterday's newspaper if some crisis came up in one of your business concerns.'

Jay ran a disturbing hand through the thick dark brown of his hair. 'If I did, it would only be because I was safeguarding our future.'

'Your future,' she corrected dully, her feet leaden in their denim casuals as she put space between herself and Jay. 'Mine lies in another direction now.'

'With the estimable ship's purser?' he jeered, but he seemed content to flare at her from across the space of the sitting room.

'At least I'd know where I stood with him! I'd have an ordinary, sane life with Rick.'

'Really? With a man who's at sea ninety-five per cent of the time?' Jay's eyes narrowed. 'Or is that the idea? A man who'll provide board and demand very little bed?'

Toni felt her cheeks flush to deep scarlet. Hadn't those been her exact thoughts any time she had seriously contemplated marrying Rick? A man simple and undemanding, who would perhaps give her children to sublimate the love she had once felt for a man of steel. Only now, under Jay's scathing eye, did she see the supreme selfishness of her thinking. Rick deserved better than that. But before she could open her mouth to speak, Jay had taken the initiative from her.

'But that's all academic now,' he said brusquely. 'Unless you want this old tub and her crew to sink into oblivion, you'll go along with my terms.'

'Which are?' she asked faintly.

'That you give this Rick the final brush-off, and that you resume relations with me as my wife.'

A dull curiosity filled the eyes she lifted to his. 'Why are you doing this, Jay? I know you, there has to be an angle.'

'Let's just say I'm saving you from a fate worse than death, which a marriage to Rick Warren would be. He's no match for a hot-blooded woman like you.'

Ignoring that, apart from a slight deepening of the flush under her tan, Toni said challengingly: 'I can't suddenly come out and tell Captain Vance and—and everybody that I'm not divorced after all. And to top it off, folks, the mysterious Mr Brownlea in Stateroom 6 is not Mr Brownlea at all but Jason Stanford, my husband!'

'All right,' Jay decided in his inimitable way, 'you don't have to tell them I'm your husband. As it happens, it suits me that no one knows who I am yet. You can tell them you've fallen suddenly, madly in love with Mr Brownlea, and he with you. How's that?'

Toni's head lifted in irritation. 'They know I'm not the kind to fall suddenly, madly in love with anyone, let alone the man who has the power to make or break the *Aztec Queen*.'

'Maybe they'll regard you as a heroine, then, one

who's willing to go above and beyond the call of duty to secure the fate of a grand old ship of the line,' he supplied obliquely.

Toni faced him, the full line of her lips compressed to tautness. 'You expect me to hop into bed with you, just like that, as if nothing had happened in between?'

'Just like that,' he nodded in confirmation.

'And what about Gloria? Isn't she expecting your undivided attention on this trip to romantic Mexico? I gathered from her surprise at seeing me that she had no idea I work on the *Queen*.' Her eyes widened in sudden comprehension. 'Or is that why you did it? You came on this trip to give Gloria the heave-ho, didn't you, using me for your barricade. Was she finally putting pressure on for you to finally get rid of me and make an honest woman of her?'

'There's never been any question of marriage between Gloria and me,' Jay said stiffly, feeling for and finding the cigarette pack in his shirt pocket. While he lit one and drew hard on it, Toni's conjectures went even further.

'Why did you suddenly stop the divorce proceedings?' she asked with deceptive mildness.

Jay shrugged and moved on bare feet across the carpet to stand at the window, where he stared moodily out at one of the ship's cruise boats ferrying passengers to shore.

'It suited me at the time.'

'I'll bet it did,' she jeered, hurt by the knowledge that had seeped into her mind. Since he had told her that she was still his wife, hope had flickered somewhere deep inside her, hope that he had changed his mind about the divorce because he couldn't bear to sever that final tie between them. Now she knew otherwise.

'Gloria's fine for a mistress,' she goaded, 'but you couldn't see her playing the role of submissive wife waiting, as I did, for you to come home to your warmed over dinner whenever you could spare the time. She would be a very demanding wife, wouldn't she, Jay?'

'Be quiet, Toni,' he returned almost wearily. 'You know nothing about the contribution Gloria's made to the Company. And yes, dammit,' he swung round savagely, 'she was always there when I needed her. Don't think I didn't need a woman's understanding lots of times when we were married, but I never took advantage of it, whatever you think. Trust never was one of your strong points, was it?'

'Neither was simple-mindedness,' she retorted sharply, then took a few steps towards the outer door. 'I have to get out of here,' she muttered as if in a message to herself.

'You can give me your answer at dinner tonight, when you'll be my guest.'

'Not on the ship,' she shot back over her shoulder. 'The crew isn't allowed to mingle socially with passengers.'

Jay strolled casually the length of the room, one brow arched sarcastically. 'I doubt if Captain Vance would object to *my* enjoyment of your charming company.' His slight emphasis on the 'my' brought Toni's teeth together in a tight clench at the reminder that the Captain would probably fall over

backwards trying to please 'Mr Brownlea'. 'But it
might be fun to eat somewhere ashore. You must
know all the best places by now.'

'Naturally.' Toni threw him a pseudo-sweet look
from the corner of her eye. 'The ban only applies on
board, and there's never any shortage of unattached
men on our cruises.'

'It's still pretty limiting, though,' he said conversationally, as if they were discussing the price of
beans. 'I mean, having to part company at the head
of the gangway after a—romantic evening ashore.'

Toni forced a laugh that was a fair imitation of
Carole's, and used the words she had heard her
cabin mate utter many times. 'When you get back
in the wee small hours, who knows or cares which
cabin you take your shoes off in?'

'I see. Well,' Jay rubbed his hands briskly together, 'suppose we meet at seven where the boats
take off for the great metropolis?'

'Do I have a choice?'

'None. I was just being polite.'

Without another word, Toni wrenched open the
door and slammed it behind her, disregarding the
unheard-of disturbance in this small and exclusive
section of the ship until a steward poked an astonished head out of the serving area. Toni recognised
him as Pearson, an Englishman like Cope but without the tact and discretion of the Captain's steward.

Pearson's face now registered intense curiosity.
He must know which stateroom she had come from,
and that the man registered as Brownlea had to be
treated with kid gloves.

'Anything wrong, miss?'

'No. The door slipped out of my hand.'

His long and lugubrious face continued to look curiously after her as she half ran to the heavy doors at one end of the wide passageway, and she knew that by nightfall it would be all over the ship that she and the important passenger she was supposed to placate had had an unholy row. 'I saw it with me own eyes,' she could hear him tell it, 'and he definitely threw her out and crashed the door behind her.'

Giving a visible shrug as she hurried down the companionway to the desk below, Toni decided that it didn't matter. By that same nightfall, she would be seen dining in Cabo San Lucas with Jay by a hundred or so passengers and not a few of the crew.

And if Jay had his way, the whole ship would know that the Assistant Cruise Director was making his nights as memorable as his days aboard the S.S. *Aztec Queen.*

The music for dancing was soft and dreamy. The dinner, part Mexican, part American style, had been superb. The *mariachi* music had been loud and plaintively devoted to the theme of love.

Everything was set for romance with a capital R, and Toni wished she could go back a year or two to the first months of her marriage to Jay. If only they could have done this then, known the magic of relaxation and moonlight on the ocean, the pulsing beat of Mexico's vibrant life, the precious oneness there could be between two people.

Her hand tightened on the cotton knit weave of Jay's navy shirt. It would have been wonderful—

then. Now, it was too late. Jay's life was planned
around what suited Jay. And none of his plans had
ever taken into account *her* feelings, *her* needs.
From the beginning, she had had to take a back seat,
with business as his co-driver. It could never be any
other way with Jay, despite his promises of acting
only in a supervisory capacity. To go back to him as
his wife would only mean more of the same heartache. And that she couldn't take more than once in
a lifetime.

'Why, Toni!' an astonished Carole trilled as she
danced by with the stalwart Mike, her light blue
eyes avidly devouring Jay's well-set figure in navy
shirt and cream slacks that clung to his flat hips as
if grown there. 'You didn't say you were coming
here tonight.'

'Neither did you,' Toni retorted drily, thankful
when Jay manoeuvred her away from the frankly
curious Carole. Their meeting in the cabin had
been brief at six, each hurrying to shower and trans-
form herself into radiant beauties of the evening.
That they had succeeded was evident in Mike's
adoring hold on Carole's tomato red chiffon dress
that made her blonde head stand out in statuesque
beauty; and Jay's hand had crept up over the smooth
brown of Toni's bare back to lodge warmly against
her nape.

He had always done that, she reflected dreamily,
as if he sensed that her security sprang from that
particular spot. She had to force all her powers of
concentration on what he was murmuring now at
her ear.

'Remember that week at the lake cottage? When

I supplemented our meagre supplies of steaks with fish from the lake?'

Toni lifted her head from his shoulder indignantly. 'You did not! If we'd had to rely on your fishing catch we'd have starved to death!'

'Oh, well, my memory's not too good in that area.' His smile faded to seriousness when he drew her head back to his shoulder, then murmured: 'But I do remember very clearly how we made love on the beach with the water lapping at our feet.'

Toni closed her eyes helplessly, lost in the powerful surge of longing that made her sag dependently on the firm strength of Jay's body. How well she remembered the fierce, sudden passion that had overtaken them and left them gasping on the sand. The sand had been damp, cold, but Jay had warmed her entire body in the heat of their coming together. Then, the following morning——

'They called you from your office the next morning, didn't they?' she challenged with a lift of her head, strength flowing back into her limbs. 'No, not *they*—— Gloria. We couldn't even have one week alone together.' Tears studded her eyes to diamond brilliance. 'Was that too much to ask? One lousy week in a whole year?'

'It was an important deal, darling,' he placated patiently. 'Gloria did what she thought was best.'

Toni broke from his hold and went unsteadily to their table. Jay, she knew, would think her swaying step was due to the wine they had drunk, the aperitifs before dinner. But it wasn't. All the old traumas had descended on her like a wet blanket again, submerging her in a misery she already knew to its bitter depths.

'I want to go back to the ship.'

'Let's have some coffee first.' Jay signalled to a waiter, who came immediately to fill their cups with the faintly acrid brew. Toni drank hers black, and found it did little to ease the weight of her depression, but it did clear her brain enough to know that Jay was once more masterminding her.

Cursing herself for her foolishness in letting him think that she made a habit of coming late to the ship and pairing off with whichever man she happened to be with, her mind began to think in clear, practical terms. She knew every nook and cranny of the *Queen*, so it would be a simple matter for her to evade Jay once they were on board.

Simple, yes. What would be hard would be the fight against her own instincts to submit to the pull of her senses and go willingly with Jay to his stateroom, to know again the hard thrust of his body, the tenderness in his sinewy arms. He evidently wanted it, and God knew that she did too.

But what about afterwards, when the call of business would make him set her aside abstractedly, a toy to be picked up at the whim of its owner? And set down twice as fast.

Toni watched as the lights of the ship grew closer. She was grateful, in spite of the cosy feel of her wool wrap, for the warm bulk of Jay behind her, the encompassing protection of his arms around her. If only ... if only....

Her entire life seemed bounded by those two nostalgic words. Useless words, denoting as they did things that might have been, yet could never be. Just like a leopard who was powerless to change his spots, so was Jay unable to alter the abiding passion of his life, business. There would always be another deal to absorb his interest.

'I'll make a deal with you, Jay,' she said in the kind of language he understood as she ran lightly up the steps hugging the ship's side. 'If you can find me, you can have me.'

'Toni?'

The constrained bewilderment in his voice was like an added impetus to her feet, which winged their way familiarly over decks and up stairways in a maze that brought her up short, panting, at a point beyond the forward funnel. The space here was reserved for the crew on their off-duty time, and it was unlikely Jay would find her here.

Was she glad, or sorry? Toni weighed the twinkling lights of Cabo San Lucas on her left with the dark vastness of black sea to her right.

The trembling ache at the pit of her stomach told her she was sorry . . . very sorry. Her mind held memories of a different kind, and it was these she must hold to.

CHAPTER FOUR

SHE was up before six the next morning, surprised that she had slept so well. Carole's bed was unruffled, so it was a certain bet that she had spent the night with Mike. There was nothing in this to shock Toni now. From the little Carole had told her about her marriage, she could understand the fair girl's aversion to the institution.

Yet was she really happy, hopping from man to man and bed to bed? There was that feverish kind of searching for an available male at the beginning of each trip, the deep depression when no one presentable showed up. Then she threw herself into her work, to the point where Toni felt herself unnecessary at times. Wouldn't she be happier in a permanent relationship, without all the uncertainties of chance?

It would never do for her, Toni, but, she shrugged as she stepped under the shower, it was none of her business. She had told Carole even less about her own marriage, and the other girl had never pried. The least she could do was to return the compliment.

The great ship's engines were already churning in a deep throb when she emerged on deck minutes later, dressed to take the exercise class at seven. There was a tacit understanding between herself and Carole that Toni, as the junior member of the entertainment staff, would face the enthusiasts at an hour when she herself preferred to catch up on lost sleep. Toni liked to rise early, so she didn't mind, and it meant that she had an hour or so free in the afternoon.

Cabo San Lucas had already disappeared round the end of the bay, and the morning air was damp as Toni leaned on the rail with her elbows and watched the beginning fingers of light where the sun would shortly appear on the horizon. She loved this time of day on board, when she might have been alone on the ship if not for the deckhands sluicing the decks and singing off-key in their Portuguese accents. One of the liveliest evenings she had spent aboard had been on their mess deck when she and Carole and the other female members of the crew had been invited to celebrate some Portuguese feast day. The songs they had sung then had spoken eloquently of their homesickness for their own land, their own people.

Now as she went below in search of coffee provided by the ship for early birds, she smiled at their ribald greetings, knowing that they accepted her as a necessary part of the ship's smooth running.

Marian Lester, the assistant purser, was drawing a cup of coffee from the huge urn located amidships. ' 'Oh, it's you.'

Feeling it was too early in a fresh new day to waste time in an exchange of veiled hostility, Toni filled her own cup and followed the other girl to one of the deck tables lining the rail.

'I'm afraid I'm one of those people who are at their best in the early morning hours,' she said with a rueful smile as she set her cup down opposite Marian's and pulled out a chair.

Marian stared down into the cup she was stirring automatically. 'I'd have thought you'd be—otherwise occupied this morning.'

'Really?' Toni stared at the other girl, whose appearance was the same as always. Hair scraped back into an apology for a French twist, face innocent of make-up, a mustard-coloured blouse doing nothing at all for her sallow complexion. 'What makes you think that?'

'You were with Mr Brownlea last night.' Marion took a deep gulp of her coffee. 'Rick and I saw you.'

Toni's eyes widened in genuine amazement. Not because Marian had noticed her with Jay, but that she had been with Rick. Suddenly it hit her that they would make a perfect couple. Marian and Rick. They were of the same type, correct in their manner and—yes, slightly prudish in their outlook.

'You were with Rick last night?'

'Is there anything wrong with that?' Marian bristled defensively.

'No, of course not.' Toni thought rapidly. It would solve the problem of Rick if he could see herself differently, Marian in a clearer light. 'I'm glad you were with him.'

'Thanks, Lady Bountiful,' the other girl returned sourly. 'I guess it's nothing to somebody like you to drop one man when a richer one appears on the horizon.'

'It isn't that way, Marian. There's never been anything—serious between Rick and me.'

'Try telling him that!' The words were torn from

a deep-seated anguish, and Toni stared across the table miserably.

'He tried to pretend he was enjoying the evening with me, but I could tell he was eaten up with jealousy over you. I could have been a fossilised fish for all the attention he paid to me!'

Toni looked perplexedly into the other girl's eyes. She could be attractive, if only she had a little know-how in feminine artifice. Her hair could be cut and styled in a flattering way, her sallow skin brought to more vibrant life with the skilful use of cosmetics, and warm hues, which could bring colour to her skin, in her clothes.

'Marian, I—I'm very fond of Rick. He's a won-derful guy, kind, considerate, everything a girl could ask for, but——' Toni's eyes dropped to where her finger described a circle round the rim of her cup. 'You see, I'm still in love with my hus-band, and I'll never be able to love any other man in that particular way.'

Now what had made her confess to Marian, a girl who had every reason to loathe and envy her, the truth she had been avoiding in her own mind? Oh, she had thought she was getting over Jay, apart from the odd leap of her pulses when she saw a man who resembled him, but the untruth of that had been evident from her first glimpse of him on board ship, his first touch, the kiss that had set her pulses ham-mering. But how could Marian be expected to un-derstand those things? She had never known the kind of love that drew a man and a woman together in a web of steel that was impossible to break.

Then Marian surprised her by saying diffidently:

'I—think I know what you mean. I'd feel the same if I'd been married to Rick and—oh *damn*! Why did I say a thing like that?'

'Because you meant it, I guess,' Toni said gently, amazed at her sudden sense of kinship with the other girl. Her deep brown eyes were warm as they went over Marian's face and hair. 'I know it's not supposed to make any difference these days, but it's amazing the amount of confidence a woman can get from a new hairdo, a new shade of lipstick. Why don't you try it?'

'I wouldn't know how to start,' Marian frowned gloomily.

'Maybe not, but Donna in the beauty salon knows a lot about hair, and I could help you with the make-up bit.'

Marian eyed her suspiciously. 'Why should you?'

'Let's just say I think Rick deserves somebody like you, a girl who really cares for him.'

'I'll think about it,' Marian said abruptly, and rose without another word to carry her empty cup back to the serving table.

Oh, well, Toni shrugged mentally, she shouldn't expect miracles—and she shouldn't be trying to plan other people's lives for them. Lingering for a few minutes, she listened to the hiss of the white-frothed green water far below as the *Queen* sliced her way towards the next stop, Mazatlan.

Several beach and lunch parties had been arranged, she and Carole splitting up to supervise two of them. This wasn't strictly necessary, but Captain Vance liked a ship's representative on hand in case of problems in the smooth running of the shore-based operation.

More people were milling about the deck now, and Toni exchanged pleasantries with several on her way to the sun deck above. White skins unused to the heat were beginning to tan, some painfully so. It happened on every cruise, no matter how many warnings were issued by the Ship's Bulletin, a news sheet delivered early each morning to the cabins. Most of Dr Mackenzie's patients consulted him for just that reason.

Her exercise group, somewhat depleted, was gathered in the area between funnels. This, too, happened on each sailing. Too fervent enthusiasm at the beginning gave way gradually to the late nights and torpor of Mexico's heat. Toni shed her sweat suit and stood slim and straight before them, flashing them a brilliant smile as she said:

'Good morning! And congratulations to the few of you who made it out of bed! Let's begin with a few warming up exercises, then we'll get on to the big stuff.'

The session progressed, with the exercises becoming gradually more strenuous, until a rangy middle-aged Texan panted:

'Honey, if—you—weren't such—a pretty—little gal, I'd—never do this—again.'

'Oh, come on now, Mr Branch,' Toni retorted, her breathing scarcely altered, 'we're still just warming up.'

'Well,' he drawled, standing upright and relaxing his long arms by his sides, 'maybe you are, honey, but I reckon I'm as warm as I'm going to get.'

The heart had gone out of the group by this time, and Toni called an end to the session, reminding them as they went thankfully down to breakfast,

'There won't be any more exercise sessions until after Mazatlan, but I'll be very happy to see any or all of you then.'

Left alone, she walked to where she had thrown her sweat suit, and was pulling on the thick trousers when a voice from the deck above, the Bridge Deck, called down mockingly:

'Don't pin your hopes on seeing any of that bunch of deadbeats again!'

Squinting her eyes upward, Toni saw Jay in immaculate whites leaning negligently on the open part of the Bridge rail. For a moment she teetered dangerously, half in and half out of the pants, then her melting backbone firmed and she finished drawing them on, reaching then for the matching red top with its two vertical white side stripes.

She paused momentarily under Jay's mocking glance to throw up briefly: 'I doubt if Captain Vance would appreciate your calling passengers "deadbeats"—and at least they had the gumption to get up and out this morning!'

'If that's a dig at me, it's unjustified. I did fifty push-ups before seven.'

'Congratulations,' Toni tossed up sourly. It was probably true.

Jay had always kept himself superbly fit, despite the calls on his time during the day. The squash court he had had installed in the basement of the Stanford building was used by him more than anyone, and he encouraged his staff to do the same.

'If you'll excuse me,' she said with sweet sarcasm, 'I'm going to breakfast now.'

'Have it with me.'

'No, thanks. I eat at the staff table. Jay?' Her voice rose to a squeak as he lifted one long leg and hitched it over the rail, bringing over the rest of his body until he hung by his hands between decks. 'What do you think you're doing?'

Her eyes widened in horror when he let go and dropped to the deck on rubber-soled shoes. A second later he was walking lightly across to stand facing her, a faint gleam of sarcastic amusement lighting the cool grey of his eyes.

'Don't look so worried, sweetheart, it was just a little drop.'

Toni's breath caught in sudden ire. 'You can splatter yourself all over the deck for all I care,' she snapped. 'It just isn't the kind of publicity we want for the *Queen*.'

His brows rose a fraction. 'Nasty! You never used to be that way.'

'I've learned how the hard way.' Toni made to go past him. 'Now if you'll excuse me, I have a full pro-gramme this morning.'

'Toni, wait.' Amazingly there was appeal in the broad hand he laid on her forearm. 'I want to talk to you about—last night, and other things.'

'You did all your talking in the cabin the other day.' She pulled her arm away from his hold so that his hand dropped to his side. 'A lot of talk that amounted to blackmail. You've become pretty nasty yourself, Jay.'

His eyes narrowed to steel slits. 'I could have been a lot nastier last night after you ran away from me, but I wasn't, was I?'

'Only because you didn't know where to find me!'

'Didn't I?' he questioned softly, then his hand shot out again to clamp around her wrist. 'Would you like me to show you where you were?'

Without ceremony, he dragged her across the intervening space between funnels and beyond to the enclosed space reserved for the crew.

'Well?' he demanded grimly.

Toni frowned and looked back. They were completely hidden from human view. 'But how——?'

'I haven't exactly been wasting my time on lazy shipboard pursuits. You should have remembered how thoroughly I go over something before investing a lot of money in it. I probably know more about the layout of this ship than you've picked up in all the time you've been on her.'

'That I don't doubt!' Toni looked up at him then, puzzled. Her eyes glanced quickly off his and up to where the wind teased at his dark hair, ruffling it boyishly on his forehead.

There were still signs of workaday strain around his eyes and mouth, but they were less now than when he came aboard. Even he had to relax his deathlike grip on the reins of business, surrounded as he was by the carefree air of shipboard life.

'If you—knew where I was, then why didn't you——?'

'Why didn't I come after you and take you by force?' he supplied caustically, then his voice softened to a kind of tenderness. 'Because that's not the way I want it to be between you and me. It was never a forced issue before, and I don't want it to be now. And I know it doesn't have to be.'

The sun glinted across his eyes, turning them into pale orbs of burning silver.

'You're very sure of yourself, aren't you?'

'Where you're concerned, yes.' His arms came round her and drew her lifeless body to him. Looking down into her face, he said huskily:

'Want me to show you that, too?'

Toni was incapable of resisting the steady pressure at her back that brought her to the rock-hard outline of Jay's body and forced her head up to meet the descending line of his mouth. His lips moved gently, persuasively, disarming her completely and stirring the old embers of a passion which she knew now would never die between them. Jay knew it as instinctively as she did, so where was the point in trying to resist?

Her hands crept up over the blood-warm contours of his chest and joined together again behind his head. His hair was cool and windblown between her fingers, his skin warmly scented from the aftershave he had always used.

The lift of his head was leisurely when the windborne sound of voices reached them.

'Jay ...' Toni whispered shakily, then leaned her forehead on the taut white knit of his shirt. 'I—I couldn't go through all that again.'

He seemed to know exactly what she meant. His fingers groped for and found her chin, then raised it until her mournful eyes looked directly into his.

'I've told you, you won't have to go through that ever again. I know it was rough on you, honey, but there was nothing I could do about it—then. Now, things are nearly plain sailing, and I'm going to devote myself exclusively to you.'

Toni blinked and broke the mesmeric spell that bound her eyes to his. Shaking her head, she slid

her hands down across his shoulders until they
rested on his muscled upper arms.

'How could that be, Jay? Business is your life,
you'd die without it.'

'*You're* my life—and I'll prove it to you. No, let me
finish. I'll make a deal with you,' Jay mocked her
own words of the previous night. 'I won't ask for a
commitment from you until you're ready to give
one. All I do ask is that you wipe the slate clean of
the past and let me win you all over again. Will you
do that?'

Pushing away the small voice that spoke from
bitter depths, Toni nodded wordlessly. No words
were possible through her emotion-choked throat,
the deep thunder of her heart. All that mattered
was that Jay wanted her, had said '*You're* my life' as if
he really meant it.

He was kissing her again now, as if he meant that,
too, but then he lifted his head and clutched a
handful of her sweat suit top, cursing softly before
he said:

'This must be the most unsexy garment known to
man!'

Laughter bubbled suddenly, joyfully to her lips.

'It was designed by a woman to discourage male
predators.'

Jay's face sobered as his hand lifted to stroke back
a strand of hair from her forehead. 'Don't try to
discourage me any more—please?'

Toni shook her head, her eyes reflecting the deep
shine of happiness. If Jay noticed the hesitancy
lurking behind the joyful sheen, he ignored it as he
bent to kiss the tip of her nose lightly.

'Okay. You'd better go about your duties now. But I'm going to fix it with the Captain that you eat at my table for dinner.'

It was as she skipped lightly down the five sets of stairs to her own deck that Toni remembered Gloria. Was there to be an uncomfortable three-some at the table that night?

Carole rushed into the cabin as Toni was leaving it. The fair girl's blue cocktail dress from the evening before looked tawdry in the morning light, and she eyed Toni's white uniform top and pleated skirt with a jaundiced eye.

'Why do you always look so fresh and virtuous?' she complained, kicking off her sandals as she walked to the dressing table they shared.

Toni looked back at her from where she stood with one hand on the doorknob.

'Good morning to you, too! How did it go?'

'How did what go?' Carole said irritably, reaching for the zipper at the back of her dress.

'Mike,' Toni returned evenly.

The other girl shrugged. 'He's all right. The only problem is his guilt complex—in this day and age.' She stepped out of the dress and wrapped a pink robe around her. 'He thinks because I spent the night with him he has to marry me.'

'Would that be so bad?'

'Oh, for heaven's sake, Toni, don't you start on me too! My life style suits me just fine—in fact,' she paused on her way to the bathroom and gave Toni an unfriendly look, 'it wouldn't do you one bit of harm to live a little yourself.'

'I'm all right as I am.'

Carole's eyes narrowed as they went over Toni's face.

'Normally,' she said slowly, 'I wouldn't agree with you, but there's something different about you this morning. It wouldn't be anything to do with your date last night with the *Aztec Queen*'s prime male passenger, would it?'

'He just asked me to go ashore with him because he was alone,' Toni replied carefully. It was too soon to confide, even in Carole, that Jay was her husband and that they were probably going to get together again.

Carole was sceptical. 'A man like that needing a girl to take pity on him? Come on, Toni. What about the blonde leopard he's with?'

'He's not *with* her, actually. She's—his office aide.'

'A likely story,' Carole scoffed. 'Any time I see them around the ship, she's glued to his side like a limpet and sends out warning flashes with her eyes to any female who comes within touching distance.' She turned her head to say over her shoulder: 'Admittedly, she had a notebook and pen in hand. And now, if you'll excuse me, I'm going to make myself part of the human race again.'

'Will you be taking the lecture on Mazatlan?' Toni called to her retreating back.

'Of course. You can do the Puerto Vallarta one. Meanwhile, maybe you can organise the tickets for the Mazatlan bus tours for the onslaught after the lecture. I'll get down there to help as soon as I can.'

Toni went to breakfast, and an hour later was behind the Entertainments counter in the main lobby, lining up tickets for the various bus tours on the low inner counter. Then she crossed the hall to where Rick was stationed at the Purser's desk.

'Hi, Rick,' she told his bent head brightly.

'Oh—good morning, Toni.'

As he straightened, she saw lines of disapproval etching his clearly marked features, and her heart sank slightly inside her. She was fond of Rick—had even contemplated marrying him—and she hated the thought of bad feeling between them.

'May I have the float cash for bus tickets?'

'Certainly.' Rick turned away without another word and came back moments later with a black cash box.

'Try to get it right this time when you return it, will you?'

Toni stared at him in shock. Balancing the money for the tickets and returning the float cash intact had never been her strong point, but always before Rick had goodhumouredly and speedily sorted it out for her. Now he was looking across the counter as if she were a stranger, and one he didn't like very much.

'I'll do my best,' she said stiffly, and had turned away when Rick called after her:

'Enjoy your date with a passenger last night?'

Toni swung back on her heel to look at him again, angry colour reddening her skin under the tan.

'Yes, thanks. Did you?'

'I wasn't with a passenger. It's against company regulations, you know.' His stony face flickered contempt at her, and Toni took a step towards the counter, lowering her voice as a group of passengers came noisily into the hall.

'Mr Brownlea is a very special kind of passenger, as *you* well know.'

'He was certainly special to you, I could see that with no trouble.'

'And wasn't Marian special to you?'

His eyes dropped from the wrath in hers.

'That's different.'

'So was my date with Mr Brownlea!' Toni whirled and stomped back to her own side of the hall, her hands shaking as she counted out the money into separate piles. She had counted it several times before the realisation dawned that Rick had given her ten dollars short.

Glancing up, perplexed, her eyes met Rick's. A small, tight smile flickered round his mouth before he turned his back deliberately. He had done it purposely! But why? So he could act superior when she went back to adjust the error?

Her mouth firmed into a stubborn line. She would never give him that satisfaction, even if she had to replace the money from her own purse.

The onslaught, as Carole had described it, seemed larger and more pushy than normal, despite reassurances that there would be plenty of space on most of the tours. By the time everyone had been satisfied, both she and Carole were exhausted, their nerves frayed.

'Sorry to leave you to cash up, Toni,' Carole said wearily, 'but I have to check up on the rehearsal for tonight's show. Anna wants to try something different tonight.'

Toni was still struggling with the piles of notes and credit card slips half an hour later, so hopelessly lost in the intricacies of balancing the books that she was oblivious even to Rick's watchful presence directly across the hall.

'What in the name of all that's holy are you trying to do?'

The familiarity of the voice made her head jerk up, and she was conscious suddenly of how her lipstick had disappeared and that her short-styled hair must be standing on end from the times she had run despairing fingers through it.

'Oh—Jay!' Her cheeks flooding with colour, she gestured to the chaos before her. 'Just balancing up the cash.'

'*Balancing* it, or moving it round from one pile to another?'

Toni bit her lip. 'I'm not very good with money.'

'You never were,' Jay said briskly, opening the side gate and stepping through to stand beside her. 'Let me see if I can help you.'

'Oh, Jay, I don't think you should. I mean, it's not right——'

'Of course it's right. The sooner you're through here, the sooner you'll be free to have coffee with me.'

Marvelling at his ability to apply his expertise to such small amounts when he was used to thinking in millions, Toni was content to let him take over.

In no time at all, the ticket stubs for each tour were banded with the money and set aside. She was so absorbed in watching the deft way his fingers flipped through the notes, and re-confirming the surprising length of his lashes as he bent, frowning, over the counter that she completely forgot her intention to replace the missing ten dollars from her own money.

'How much did you say should be in the box?' he asked, turning his head suddenly to look disconcertingly into her bemused eyes.

'Oh. I know about the missing ten dollars,' she stammered, reaching for her purse.

'What in hell are you doing?' Jay took the purse from her and threw it back on the table behind them. 'Why is there ten dollars missing?'

'It was—a m-mistake.' Her eyes involuntarily strayed across the hall to where Rick had returned to his post, his brow glowering at them across the space. Jay's eyes followed hers, and his mouth tightened to an angry line.

'Please let me put it back, Jay, I'll sort it out later.'

'We'll sort it out right now!' he snapped, taking up the black cash box and the bag containing the tour receipts and striding across the hall to where Rick stood with stubbornly set jaw. Toni followed, wishing miserably that Jay had let her fix things in her own way. As it was, Rick would believe she had enlisted Jay to fight the battle for her.

'There was a ten-dollar deficit when you handed this over to my—to Miss Morelli.'

'That's not possible, sir,' Rick returned stonily, the slight pause before 'sir' indicating adroitly his question as to what business it was of a passenger. 'I check all the cash myself.'

'Then you'd better check it all again, to find out where the missing money is.'

'I take orders like that only from Captain Vance. Certainly not from one of the passengers'—he paused again—'no matter who he is.'

Jay's jaw hardened, his eyes mere slits of steel.

'I'll be more than happy to bring the matter to the Captain's attention.'

The two men held each other's eyes for a full minute, one set resentfully stubborn, the other aggressively dominating. Rick's were the first to drop.

'There's no need to bother the Captain with a trivial sum like that. I'll see that it's replaced.'

'Replaced,' Jay mused. 'That means to put back something that was taken, doesn't it?'

Rick shrugged. 'If you like.'

'I do like. What I won't like is discovering that Miss Morelli has been hampered in her duty this way in future.'

'Miss Morelli won't be bothered in *any* way by me in future.' Rick's contemptuous gaze flicked over to Toni's stricken face.

'Good,' Jay said silkily, then turned to Toni. 'Coming for that coffee?'

'You go ahead. I'll join you in the Seaview Lounge in a minute.' As soon as Jay's tall form had disappeared from the hall, she turned to Rick.

'Rick, I'm sorry about this. I'd no intention of——'

'Save the pretty speeches for Mr Wonderful,' Rick said savagely, picking up the box and bag of ticket receipts, turning back to say more quietly: 'I wouldn't have thought you were the kind to jump all over a guy because he's rich and powerful. It just goes to show what a poor judge of character I am!'

'But, Rick, he's my——'

'Oh, Purser, you're just the man I want to see,' a booming male voice sounded across the hall, and Toni, after a last appealing look to Rick, who ignored it, walked out of the lobby.

She had almost blurted out that Jay was her husband. Well, why not? Because it would make her job aboard the *Queen* impossible, that's why, she told herself savagely. Everything would be changed. She wouldn't be regarded as one of the crew any more, their knowledge that she was the potential owner's wife drastically changing their attitude to her. They would close ranks against her—oh, not unkindly, but in a way that would inevitably make her aware of the huge gulf between them suddenly. From cramped two-berth cabin to luxury suite in one easy movement.

Too easy, she thought as she entered the forward lounge where tables were arranged inside full-length windows to give an unimpeded view of the sea on three sides. Jay was seated at a table to one side of the front section, and rose when she approached.

'I've ordered coffee and pastries,' he announced, seating her with the sleek dexterity he had learned on his way to the top.

'What happened?'

'With Rick? Nothing. I—nearly told him we were married.'

'What stopped you?'

She stared at him. 'Don't you realise how difficult it would be for me if everybody knew we were still married? They'd cut me out, I wouldn't be one of them any more.'

'And that would bother you?'

'Of course it would!' she cried in exasperation. 'How can I do my job properly if everybody treats me with kid gloves? Besides,' she looked down at her hands twisted together on the table before her, 'they're like—like family to me. I'd hate it if that was no longer so.'

'Nothing has to change.' Jay spoke softly, covering her hands with one of his and squeezing gently. 'We can be discreet about it when we want to be together. No one else need know. That's only for this trip, of course,' he added with a frown. 'As soon as we get back to L.A., I'll want you to be my full-time wife again—if that's what you want,' he tacked on hastily as her eyes threw a warning.

Toni's anger died as quickly as it had been born. 'I—I think I want to be your wife again, Jay, but——' She stopped and pulled at the soft outline of her lower lip with her small white teeth.

'You're still worried that I'll neglect you for business again? It can't happen, Toni. There's nothing —well, I'll be honest and tell you that there's one deal I want to put through personally, but once that's tied up, everything should be plain sailing.'

He looked expansively around the rapidly filling lounge. 'I'm beginning to like the feeling of having nothing to do, nothing to think about. No radios, television, phones.'

Toni decided not to remind him of the radiotelephone connection to the United States. She change the subject instead.

'I'm not sure about dinner tonight,' she began. 'Captain Vance——'

'It's all fixed,' Jay interrupted, breezily confident. 'Hyram has given his permission for you to join us for dinner.'

Hyram? *Us?* Resentment flickered in Toni's dark expressive eyes. Jay was manipulating things—her —in a way that was offensive to the hard-won independence she had worked for during the past two years. He had obviously discussed her with the Captain as if her own participation was unimportant.

'I could have spoken for myself,' she said hotly, sitting back abruptly when the white-jacketed waiter brought their coffee and pastries.

When he had gone, Jay leaned earnestly across the table, his expression as contrite as a man like him could manage.

'I'm sorry, Toni, I just wanted to save you from that kind of hassle. As it was, the Captain took some persuading. I believe he thought I wanted to ravish you right there at the dinner table!'

His smile was so infectious that Toni felt her own mouth quirk in response.

'He's like a ferocious mother hen defending her chick where you're concerned,' he added, a half questioning note in his voice.

Toni picked up her cup and sipped at the piping hot coffee.

'He was one of my father's best friends in Seattle, and he's kept a fatherly eye on me ever since I came to work on the ship.'

Jay frowned as he stirred sugar into his coffee. 'He knows about our marriage?—my real name?'

Toni nodded. 'He knows I was married to a man

called Stanford. He thinks we're divorced.' She reached for one of the still-warm pastries.

'He doesn't know that you and Brownlea are one and the same, though.' Changing the tack, she asked lightly: 'Who are the "us" dining together tonight? Are we at the Captain's table?'

Jay's hesitation was only momentary, then he said briskly: 'No. Gloria and a fellow called Cyrus Jackson are making up a foursome.'

'Really!'

'It wasn't of my choosing,' he told her quietly, signalling for the waiter to refill the cup he had emptied in two draughts.

'You mean Gloria also decides who you'll have at your table?' mocked Toni tersely.

'For God's sake, Toni, she came on this cruise as my working partner! I can't just drop her and leave her to her own devices because——'

He bit the words off with a tight compression of his lips, and Toni filled the gap.

'Just because you happened to meet up with your ex-wife—pardon me, your wife?' Her cup rattled against the saucer as she replaced it.

'I didn't just happen to meet up with my wife,' he gritted impatiently. 'I came on this cruise for one purpose and one purpose only—to get you back. And, so help me, I'm going to do just that if it takes every second of this voyage to do it!' His lean face glowered determinedly at her across the table.

'So you never had any intention of buying the *Queen*?'

He ran a ruffling hand through his hair. 'I wanted to look her over, yes. But you have to realise, Toni, there's a lot that needs updating about this ship if she's to be a viable commercial enterprise. She needs new stabilisers, not to mention a complete overhaul of the engine room. In the cabin area, the existing set-up would pretty well have to be torn out and replaced.'

'We never have complaints about the accommodation,' Toni said stubbornly.

'That's not surprising,' he retorted grimly. 'Most of the higher priced cabins could be made into two, they're too big. Even with increased rates, the ship would just about break even after five years or so.'

'Why does everything with you have a price tag?' Toni complained, her eyes hard as they met his.

'Because it's not my money I would be using. I have to answer to stockholders, remember.'

'So you're not going to take on the *Queen*?' she challenged after a slight pause, furious with the starting prickle of tears at the back of her eyes.

Jay reached a hand across the table and squeezed hers, saying softly: 'I didn't say that. But the whole thing has to be gone over pretty thoroughly before I can make any kind of commitment, you know that. Gloria hardly takes a minute off, working on facts and figures most of the day.'

'I'll bet she does,' Toni said pettishly, pulling her hand out from under his. 'If she knows it's something I want, she'll make the picture look as black as possible!'

'You're wrong about Gloria,' he frowned. 'She accepts that I want us to be together again.'

'Isn't that big of her?' she mocked sweetly.

Jay's jaw hardened. 'Look, I'm not saying she

would have turned me down if I'd wanted things that way,' he said bluntly. 'She's an attractive woman, and she hardly ever goes out with any of the many men who ask her. In fact,' he paused and looked down into his cup, 'I've sometimes thought it might be a good idea if we teamed up. We work well together in business, but——'

'That's hardly the same as having a pocket calculator in bed with you, is it?' Toni flared, hiding the pain that had suddenly shot through her.

'Cut it out, Toni! You never used to be this vindictive.' The flash of steel in his grey eyes sobered to a slate colour. 'I was about to say that I couldn't do it because she wasn't you.'

Toni looked away from the accusation in his eyes. Would it ever be any different between them? It had been only a few days since they had met again, yet here they were back in the old routine of bickering—and about the same things: Gloria and his business commitments.

'I'll get rid of her, if that's what you want,' Jay pursued quietly. 'It wouldn't be hard. I'm not the only one who appreciates her head for business. She's had a lot more offers over the years than she's ever told me about.'

But I'd like to bet she made darned sure that he knew about the more important ones, Toni thought viciously, then gave an inward sigh. Having Jay get rid of Gloria would cause more problems than it would solve. For one thing, the other woman would have the smug satisfaction of knowing that Toni was behind it, that she feared Gloria's powerful influence over Jay.

'That isn't necessary,' she said, rising to her feet. 'It's a long cruise, and a lot of things could happen by the end of it. Or not happen,' she stressed, looking up into Jay's bland expression as he stood up too.

'They will,' he said softly, his hand curving firmly round her elbow. 'We're meant to be together, Toni, and you know it. If this wasn't a public room. I'd prove it to you again.'

Reminded of the filled tables around them, Toni glanced guiltily round the immediate vicinity and found several pairs of curious eyes fixed on herself and Jay.

'I have to go and arrange the bingo for after lunch,' she said hurriedly, and Jay dropped his hand.

'Okay. Will you come up to the stateroom for drinks around seven?'

Toni nodded, then wended her way through the tables, forcing herself to chat and smile normally to the several passengers who stopped her on the way.

It was the best way in the world to forget the soft melting of her insides every time she was with Jay, whether or not they were quarrelling or giving in to the dynamic attraction they felt for each other. She felt herself to be like a moth being drawn into deadly flame that would devour it.

CHAPTER FIVE

CYRUS JACKSON saved the evening for Toni with his light, self-deprecating banter. He was shorter than Jay, with thick grey hair and twinkling blue eyes behind dark-rimmed glasses, and he had long ago given up the battle against an expanding waistline.

Gloria, an aloof figure in cool green silk, shared the settee with him and looked bored in an icy way. Jay, in white tuxedo, looked more handsome and commanding than any one man had a right to be, and Toni swallowed hard when he came across to the easy chair she sat in and handed her the shallow cocktail glass, saying in a husky undertone:

'You look fantastic in that dress. Virginal white, yet your eyes would lure a monk from his cell.'

Recovered, Toni glanced up at him from under sooty lashes. 'Quite a triumph for a woman, I imagine,' she murmured.

'Don't try it,' he warned softly, and moved back to the small bar.

'If I'd been as good-looking as this guy a few years ago,' Cyrus nodded in Jay's direction, 'I'd never have made it to where I am today. I'd have been married with a passel of kids to bring up, and we all know what that can do to a man's career! He's so concerned with mumps and measles and schools and P.T.A. that in the end he doesn't really give a damn if A. T. & T. goes up or down. To make it, you have to be single-minded.'

Jay's eyes met Toni's briefly, then he turned to hand Gloria her cocktail. A long length of slender leg was visible under the thigh high slash of her dress.

'I agree,' she said after slanting a smile of thanks to Jay. 'A man should get himself established before branching out into other areas.'

'Isn't fatherhood an area for younger men?' Toni found herself saying. 'By the time he's established in a business sense, it could be too late for him to take his turn walking an infant in the middle of the night.'

'A man who's made it in business can afford to hire people to do that,' Gloria deprecated, turning away with raised eyebrows.

'I think it's important for him to have intimate personal contact with his children,' Toni insisted stubbornly, and Cyrus Jackson backed her up.

'You're right,' he nodded benignly. 'It's good for a man to marry early and have a family while he's still young enough to take part in their upbringing. I've built myself quite a fortune,' he went on with a rueful smile, 'but I have no kids to pass it on to. Pity a man can't seem to have it both ways.'

'There I disagree,' Gloria put in, sliding one shapely leg over the other. 'If I had a fortune at my disposal, I'd invest it and live high off the interest.'

'Living high isn't much fun when you have to do it alone,' Cyrus retorted plaintively, a faint twinkle in his blue eyes belying the self-pitying statement.

Gloria eyed him speculatively. 'Come on, now. You're not trying to tell us that there haven't been a million women who'd love to help you have a good time.'

Cyrus laughed delightedly. 'If there were, I couldn't have had my glasses on when they were around!' Half jokingly, he took Gloria's hand in his. 'Would you care to fill the bill temporarily?'

'Oh, well, I——' Flustered, Gloria looked round to where Jay still stood by the small bar, drink in hand. Toni's eyes went in the same direction, and her breath trapped itself in her throat when her gaze met Jay's fixed broodingly on herself.

Gloria evidently saw the same thing, because she turned back immediately to Cyrus and said in a higher pitched voice than usual: 'Why not? I seem to be at a loose end myself.'

Dinner was a difficult affair, with Gloria providing a feverish overlay to Jay's unnaturally contained silence, Toni's absorption in the scene around them, and Cyrus' contemplation of the blonde girl. Almost every sentence of Gloria's began with 'Do you remember the time, Jay, when we ...?'

To Toni's surprise, Cyrus whisked her off to dance as soon as they reached the spacious lounge three decks above. The aft full-length glass doors had been opened to permit the spill-over of dancers on to the patio bordering one of the two ship's pools. Cyrus, who danced well, guided her out there, then seemed to relax.

'You know, for years people have been telling me I should take a cruise. Now after all this time I realise how right they were. Wall Street couldn't be further away, and there's only one problem on my horizon.'

'Problem?' Toni asked abstractedly, having just noticed Jay and Gloria moving slowly together on the inside dance floor. They seemed to be having a serious conversation, standing out like sore thumbs among the uninhibited throng surrounding them. Toni returned her attention to Cyrus.

'What could possibly be bothering you on a night like this? There's a tropic moon shining on the ocean, romance in the air——'

'That's my problem right there,' he interrupted, mockingly woeful. 'There were two beautiful women at my table tonight, and both of them only had eyes for the good-looking fellow opposite me. Think I should write to one of those heartache columnists in the papers and ask what she thinks is wrong with me?'

'There's nothing wrong with you,' Toni shot back immediately, then his words sank in. Her foot missed a step, and she clung momentarily to his broad shoulders.

'What do you mean, both of us were interested in Jay?' It was fortunate, as Jay had pointed out on their way to dinner, that the missing Mr Brownlea's first name was James.

'Let's go over here and admire the moonlight for a while,' said Cyrus, releasing her right hand but keeping his on her waist as he led her to the rail. The moon spilled from the sky in a silvery reflection over the shadowy darkness of the water, an illuminating streak that moved fitfully over its surface.

'It really is something, isn't it?' He turned to look quizzically at Toni, leaning with her arms on the broad rail. 'But I guess it's old stuff to you by now. How long have you been working on the ship?'

'About two years. And yes, it really is something. I don't think I'd ever get blasé about the magic of moonlight on water.'

'You sound like a romantic,' he commented.

'What's wrong with that?'

'Not a thing. It just struck me that not all women would feel that way about it. Gloria, for instance.'

'Gloria?' she queried.

'Mm. She's crazy about that boss of hers, but she'd never think of bringing him out here to soften him up. His wife must really be something.'

'His wife?' Toni turned her head involuntarily.

'Didn't you know? He's married, so he told me. But,' he chuckled, 'that doesn't stop him admiring a pretty girl like you. He couldn't take his eyes off you all evening.'

Toni digested that in silence for a while. At least Jay hadn't hidden the fact that he had a wife, although he had let Cyrus Jackson see his open admiration for a ship's entertainment officer. The older man evidently saw nothing wrong with this.

'That's a kind of backhanded compliment,' she said briskly, pushing away from the rail, 'one I'm not interested in. He should save his admiration for his wife.'

Cyrus looked awkwardly at her, the blue-black of her hair picking up a sheen from the moon staring benignly down at them.

'I was hoping you would divert him for a while—

long enough for me to get a foothold with Gloria.'

'Gloria?' she queried.

'I know she's not the helpless, clinging variety of female,' he elaborated, somewhat sheepishly, 'but what would I do with that kind of woman anyway? Business is all I know, and she seems to understand that.'

'Oh, yes, she understands that,' Toni returned with unconscious bitterness.

Cyrus tipped his head to one side and gave her a shrewd look.

'Somehow I get the feeling that you've known her for a while. Brownlea too. Correct me if I'm completely crazy.'

Toni thought quickly. She couldn't let it get around that Jay was her husband, even via the nice Cyrus Jackson. If Gloria chose to tell him, there was nothing Toni could do about it. Up to now, the blonde woman had held her counsel, probably because Jay had asked her to, but there had been a snake-like coldness each time the pale blue eyes met hers across the table. She had seen that look there before, when Jay had sprung the surprise of their wedding on Gloria. Her fair skin had paled to alabaster, and her eyes had taken on the same hard glint.

'I—do know them, as a matter of fact,' she hesitated. 'I used to work in his office.'

'Oh? How come nobody mentioned that at dinner?' Cyrus was curious, and Toni took a few steps away from him.

'I was very low on the totem pole,' she said hurriedly. 'Look, Cyrus, I have to go inside now and check that everything's all right for the show.'

'Never off duty, huh?' he chuckled, then took her elbow to lead her back into the noisy lounge. 'Don't stay away too long, now. Your ex is finally sitting up and taking notice of you.'

'My—what?' Toni asked faintly.

'Your ex-boss,' Cyrus explained with a twinkle.

'I'm really very flattered. He's looking at me right now as if he'd like a big pit to open under my feet and sweep me out to sea.'

'I wouldn't let it bother me, if I were you,' she said lightly as she moved further into the dancing crowd, 'he doesn't have that much power.'

Not over Cyrus, perhaps, but Jay's glowering look went with her as she crossed the room and entered the small side door leading to the dressing rooms. It was as if he walked beside her, setting up a tremor in her body, a violent shaking in her knees. Two years had done nothing to change the way she felt about him. If anything, they had intensified the wordless longing she had wrapped away inside her like a cocoon.

A worried Carole was coming from the small dressing room reserved for the star. Raising her eyes heavenward in despair, she told Toni:

'The way things are at the moment, there's not going to be a show tonight.'

Toni stared at her, bewildered. 'Why on earth not? She's been a fantastic hit every evening.'

'Artistic temperament is what they call it, I believe. Merla insists people are tired of the old favourites, and she wants to try opera on them.'

'*Opera?*'

'Opera,' Carole confirmed drily. 'Seems that's what she was trained for in the dim and distant past, and she wants to do a nostalgic trip with the ship's captive audience.' A shudder rippled through her. 'If it sounds anything like it did in rehearsal this morning, the audience will jump overboard to a man.'

'Could I talk to her?' Toni said thoughtfully, remembering the long-ago evenings when she had accompanied her Italian father and various female guests in a rendition of the favourite arias.

'Be my guest,' Carole said with a resigned wave of her hand. 'Just let me know what's going to happen, if anything.'

The star of the show had thrown herself on the short settee and looked up suspiciously when Toni came in. Her heavy features had once been attractively rounded, but now they matched the seam-stretching form under a black velvet dress.

'It is of no use for you to try to persuade me,' she said plaintively in her Italian-American accent. 'I have made up my mind to sing opera, and that is what I shall do tonight, or I will do nothing at all.'

Toni sat down on the dresser stool and smiled. 'I've no intention of dissuading you, Madame Merconi. I think it's a wonderful idea.'

The heavy-lidded eyes blinked disbelievingly. 'You do?'

'Certainly. Can't I just hear you sing Puccini's *O Mio Babbino Caro*, and perhaps Verdi's *Caro Nome*?'

'Those were not my selections,' the star said doubtfully, 'I have no music for them, and those stupid musicians——' She waved a dismissing hand and quivered into injured silence.

'We don't have to bother with musicians,' Toni stated, hoping that she could remember the piano accompaniment to the well-known pieces. 'I can accompany you.'

'You?'

'Yes. I used to accompany my father and his friends. He came from Milan.'

'Ah, Milano!' The would-be prima donna beamed delightedly. '*Bene*, we will do it, you and I. The audience demands a change, I felt it last night, and what better cultural offering than the Italian operas can we give them?'

Toni cut off the impending lecture on musical appreciation for the masses, rising hurriedly and making for the door.

'If you'll excuse me, I'll go and make the arrangements.'

Carole, hovering outside the dressing room, seemed less than pleased when Toni informed her that the operatic show would go on.

'It's suicide,' she moaned. 'If you'd only heard it this morning——'

'We're not doing those,' Toni inserted hurriedly.

'We?'

'I've said I'll accompany her on the piano,' Toni explained, elaborating to the doubtful Carole: 'It's something I've done before. I just hope I can remember all the notes. For heaven's sake, Carole,' she expostulated irritably, 'it's either that or nothing.'

'Well . . . I guess we'll have to make the best of it.'

Carole said swiftly over her shoulder as she moved to the outer door. 'I'll get rid of the band and make a special announcement.'

There was no time for a display of nerves. Minutes later, Toni was following the stocky singer to the stage, which looked strangely bereft without the ship's orchestra. She took her place at the piano while Merla Merconi arranged herself beside it. Carefully, Toni avoided glancing over to where Jay sat with Gloria and Cyrus.

The numb confidence she had would dissipate rapidly under Jay's astonished look; it might have come up during their short marriage that she could play the piano, but not that she was an amateur accompanist.

Merla's doubtful nod in her direction emphasised that amateur status, and Toni's fingers seemed frozen into unnatural stiffness when she struck the first notes.

Then a strange thing happened. The ornately decorated ship's lounge faded from her consciousness and she was back once more in the double-parloured turn-of-the-century house in Seattle where she had been brought up. Her father sat just out of her line of vision, smiling, nodding, frowning when her fingers made an error.

But errors were few after the stumbling start, and Merla herself seemed to take confidence from Toni's deft blending of notes with voice, and her clever soprano flowed out over the suddenly hushed room. When the selected arias and two encores had been got through, Toni was amazed to see, on looking up from the keyboard, that much of the applause was for her. Nerves gripped her again as Merla graciously acknowledged the proficient accompaniment, and she fled unceremoniously from the small stage.

Carole caught her arm as she rushed past, awed amazement still lingering in her blue eyes. 'You were fantastic, Toni! I'd no idea you were that talented!'

Murmuring something self-deprecating, Toni made her way blindly out of the lounge that seemed noisy and stuffy all of a sudden. On deck, the air was balmy against her bare shoulders and she leaned on the rail to watch the white foam scud by far below. The long deck was deserted.

What had got into her, rushing out like that as soon as the performance had ended? Maybe it was because that night, for the first time in real depth, she had realised how much she missed her father. There would be no more happy evenings with family and friends around the piano, everyone contributing to the music except her mother, who preferred to see that there was an abundance of food and drink from her capacious kitchen.

Or maybe it was because Jay had been there, the man she loved in brain and body, but who could never give her the warm family life she had known as a girl. He didn't know how to share himself in that way. How could he? He had been orphaned at an early age and spent most of his young life in institutions where he had been treated kindly but in a sterile way. That was what had given him the driving ambition to reach the pinnacle he occupied today. Yet hadn't she loved him for those very qualities of determination and tenacity? Had she expected too much of him?

'For a girl who's the toast of the ship, you look

very sad,' Jay said quietly from her side.

Her head swivelled quickly, and she saw him through a blur of tears. Blinking them rapidly away, she gave a choked laugh.

'I guess I was thinking of when I—used to play for my father and his friends who loved singing too.'

Jay's eyes seemed opaque in the moonlight, his high cheekbones highlighting the shadowed hollows above his firm jawline. Huskily, he said: 'That's something else I didn't know about you. I'm just realising now how little I took the trouble to find out when we were together.'

Toni shrugged slightly, then said constrainedly: 'You were busy with—other things.'

'I shouldn't have been,' he stated flatly, turning to lean on the rail beside her. 'After you left, I realised how much I had neglected you.'

'But you didn't ask me to come back,' she uttered softly, knowing he would repeat the things he had said in his stateroom that first morning.

'What could I ask you to come back to?—more of the same?' He shook his head. 'It's hard to explain, but—once you reach a certain point in business, everything kind of snowballs on you. It's a self-perpetuating thing, maybe even a little scary.' He turned his head to give her a wry smile. 'It hits you all of a sudden that hundreds of people depend on you for their livelihood, and that's a sobering thought. But,' he sighed and looked seaward again, 'I shouldn't have let it interfere with our lives.'

There was a silence for the space of a few moments, then Toni said in a small voice: 'I was just thinking before you came out here that maybe I expected too much of you, that I was—selfish.'

Jay took his arms from the rail and put them round her, drawing her to him until their bodies touched lightly.

'Maybe we both were,' he said, his tone huskily low. 'But we can start again, can't we, and do a little better this time?'

'A lot better,' she corrected, smiling as his head bent and his mouth teased at the corners of hers. Her lips opened to receive the sudden hard thrust of his.

'We'll go to my cabin and continue this.'

The statement was half a question, and Toni lifted eyes that shone brilliantly in the slanting light of the moon.

'Yes,' she agreed breathily.

Grey light filtered into the stateroom and Toni stretched, languidly aware of the stiffness in her limbs. She hadn't felt so relaxed, so filled with satisfaction since she and Jay——

A smothered exclamation burst from her as she became aware of a sinewy arm curled closely around her waist, a hard male leg pressed razor-sharp against her soft calf. In the split second it took to turn her head on the pillows, her brain registered the spaciousness of the room she lay in, the long bank of dressers and wardrobes on the opposite wall.

A warm rush of remembrance flooded over her when she looked at Jay's sleeping figure beside her, his hair a ruffled mop over lean hewed features which were oddly young looking in line-erasing sleep.

They had made love, a violent, passionate love that sought to erase in minutes the deep, wordless longing of years. Jay had lost nothing of his mastery in evoking the almost painful arousal of her senses. He had been skilled, sure in his possession. So much so that ...

Toni's eyes went again over the strong outlines of his face. It was hardly likely that he had remained celibate during all the months of their separation. He wasn't the kind of man who could ignore the primitive urges of his body.

His eyes opened, puzzled at first, then essaying an upward lazy smile.

'Hi,' he said huskily, firming his arm around her and drawing her into the warm curve of his body. 'I thought I must have been dreaming.'

'You were,' she teased. 'I'm just a figment of your imagination.'

His hand went exploratively up and down her bare skin. 'You're a pretty solid figment,' he commented smugly, and settled his head with a contented sigh on her shoulder. 'What woke you so early?' he mumbled against her smooth brown skin.

'I have to go,' she said gently, running her fingers through the thick dark brown of his hair. 'I can get away with sidling through the passages now in evening dress, but——'

'I want you beside me all the time,' Jay interposed, propping himself on one elbow and looking with heavy-lidded eyes into hers. 'You're my wife, Antonia, and I want the whole world to know it.' Under his jocular tone, she sensed the male pride of possession, the need to stake his claim before all comers.

'They will,' Toni inserted softly. 'As soon as we reach L.A. Until then, I—I have to do the work I was hired to do. And I can't do that if everyone knows I'm married to you.'

'I guess I won't mind that too much,' Jay bent his head to drop a kiss near her mouth, 'as long as we can be together like this at night.' He pulled back the light covering of white sheet and traced a path with his lips from the pulsing hollow at her throat to the swelling tip of her breast.

'Jay,' she murmured against the mouth he had returned to lay lightly over hers, 'I have to go.'

'Mmm. Kiss me first,' he demanded in sudden belligerence, the darkened grey of his eyes challenging the sparkling brown of hers.

Toni's breath caught in a tangled web. How had she lived so long without him, without the living spark he imparted to every cell in her body? She loved him, had never stopped loving him. Rick might have become her husband, but he would have been nothing more than a replacement for Jay ... an inadequate replacement, she realised now in the clarity of a morning light that smudged deep shadows under Jay's cheekbones as he bent over her.

She loved him, had admitted that to herself, but what guarantee did she have that the same situation wouldn't prevail again if she returned to Chicago as his wife? It just wasn't possible that a man driven by the ambition that consumed Jay could give it all up, just like that.

But now wasn't the time to think of that, when his lips were taking a marauding course across her skin and nudging her mouth to an eager parting, his thumb stroking her taut nipples to send a new wave of desire coursing through her. Her arms circled his body and her hands, stretched to openness, ran slickly over the feline tautness of his back muscles. His responsive shudder was like a signal to her inflamed senses, and she surrendered willingly, passionately, to his thrusting demand.

Full daylight flooded the stateroom when Toni woke again. Blinking, she stared up into the long, pale face of Pearson, the Special Deck steward; his mouth had dropped to an unbecoming angle and his mud-coloured eyes had rounded in shock.

'M-Miss M-Morelli?' he stammered, steadying the coffee tray in his hand just in time.

Toni instinctively drew the sheet up to a point just below her jawbone. There could be no explanation apart from the obvious one as to her naked state in bed with a male passenger.

'Just leave the tray there,' she said huskily, nodding to the bedside table nearest her.

'Er—yes, miss.' By the time Pearson had deposited the tray and stood back to regard her through slitted eyes, his composure had returned and Toni could almost feel his haste to leave the stateroom and spread his juicy piece of scandal around the ship.

'Imagine,' she could hear him say gloatingly, 'Miss Morelli of all people!'

Now he coughed discreetly, signalling his impatience to be away. 'Will there be anything else, miss?'

'Yes,' Jay's voice rasped from behind her. 'You can get your tail out of here, and for your sake I

I hope I don't hear any gossip going around.'

Pearson put on a creditable act of being shocked. 'Certainly not, sir. I wouldn't dream of it.'

'He will,' Toni said resignedly as the door closed behind the steward.

Jay leaned on one elbow and looked down at her. 'There doesn't have to be any embarrassment for you. All we have to do is to tell them we're married.'

Toni sighed. 'I doubt if anyone would believe that. After all,' she squinted a sideways glance at him, 'you *are* travelling as Mr Brownlea, and they all think, as I did myself, that I've been divorced for quite a while.'

'I can damn soon prove who I am—and who you are!'

'No,' she said, sliding from the bed and reaching for his brown silk robe on the nearside chair, wrapping its male-size fullness round her. 'If they knew, it would make my job impossible, and I'm needed right now.'

'I need you,' Jay said starkly.

She shook her head. 'Not in the same way. The smooth running of the ship depends on me to a certain extent, but you can function very well without me.'

'Thanks.'

'Don't mention it. Besides,' she smiled at him with mock coyness, 'you've made me the ship's *femme fatale* for this trip. Every other female will be looking at me with murder in her heart.'

Leaving him frowning sourly, she walked into the bathroom, emerging seconds later to enquire: 'Can I borrow a tee-shirt and shorts from you?'

Jay, who had fallen back on his pillow, turned his head in her direction.

'Your dimensions are considerably smaller than mine,' he observed drily.

'Better I look like an undergrown schoolboy than a floozie coming back from a night on the town!'

'Where did you hear a word like that?' he posed despairingly.

'My father always used to call ladies of the night "floozies",' she returned airily, moving towards the bank of dressers on the far wall.

'May I?'

'Help yourself. Tee-shirts right ahead, shorts on your left.'

She had fished a navy cotton shirt and white drill shorts from the drawers when Jay suddenly came up behind her, stark as the day he was born.

'I need my robe,' he said, insinuating his arms around her waist and tugging at the loosely tied sash.

Toni swivelled round in his arms, her eyes darker than usual as she tilted them upward. 'Much as I'd like to stay, I have to go. Listen. What can you hear?'

He tilted his head to one side. 'Not a thing.'

'Exactly,' she affirmed crisply, sidestepping him neatly. 'That means we're docked in Mazatlan, and——' she glanced at the watch still on her wrist, 'my beach and lunch party leaves in exactly forty minutes.'

'I'll be on it.'

'You can't. You don't have a ticket.'

'Then I'll make it under my own steam. Which hotel is it?'

Toni told him, wondering if it would be a good idea for him to be in the vicinity when she was ostensibly on duty. It would be hard to keep her mind on the mundane details of supervising the beach party with Jay's distracting presence in the background. Though background was hardly the word for his presence in her life. Since their first meeting he had filled all her horizons, and she knew now that he always would.

Carole swung round from the dressing table to stare in wide-eyed amazement at Toni's loosely hanging apparel. Jay's shorts, made to fit his man-size proportions, flapped around her thighs. The navy tee-shirt mercifully covered the hip area, but the shoulder seams came far down on her upper arms.

'Where did you get that outfit?' Carole queried sarcastically, adding on a dry note: 'Or should I ask?'

Toni crossed to her own set of drawers and extracted the bikini she would wear for the beach lunch. 'No,' she said lightly, 'you shouldn't.'

'Well, I'm going to anyway. Who exchanged his shorts and shirt for your evening gown?'

'That really isn't any of your business,' Toni returned pleasantly, going to the wardrobe and selecting a pair of casual white slacks.

'The hell it isn't!' Carole exploded. 'Have you forgotten that I'm the senior member of the entertainment staff? You're answerable to me for your actions aboard ship.'

'Official actions,' Toni flared back, 'and that doesn't include where I spend my nights.'

Carole stared belligerently back at her for a moment, then bit her lip and dropped her eyes. 'Look, Toni, I know it would normally be none of my business, but—well, I feel responsible for you in a way, and I wouldn't want to think that anything I said influenced you. Yesterday,' she put to Toni's mystified eyes. 'When I said you ought to live a little, I certainly didn't mean that you should hop right into James Brownlea's bed!'

Understanding cleared Toni's brow. 'It was nothing to do with what you said,' she assured her. 'It was just—inevitable that I'd succumb one day.'

'But why him?' He's a delectable dish, granted—but I'd never have reckoned on you falling for his type. Women who'd give their all to spend a night with him, including the blonde he brought aboard, must be coming out of his ears. I've always thought you were still stuck on your ex.'

'I was—am,' Toni confirmed, unable to control the luminous shine that flooded her eyes.

'Then——?'

'Oh, Carole, can't you guess?' Keeping a secret this big would be almost impossible where her cabin-mate was concerned. 'He *is* my husband!'

Carole stared at her blankly. 'What?'

'Jay and I were never divorced,' Toni explained eagerly. 'The letter that was burned at my parents' home, the one I thought was the finalisation of the divorce, was just to tell me that Jay had suspended proceedings.'

Carole sat down with a bump on her berth. 'You mean——? You're still Mrs Brownlea?'

'That isn't his name,' Toni clarified hurriedly. 'He's really Jay Stanford.'

The blonde girl nodded with fatalistic acceptance. 'The Stanford of Stanford Industries? The brightest young star in the industrial galaxy?' At Toni's nod of agreement, Carole's eyes became suddenly sceptical. 'And he came on this trip to get you back?'

'Yes.' It was still too new and wonderful for Toni to believe it herself.

'So the old *Queen* is on her way to the scrapyards after all?'

'No! Jay's been looking into it, that's why he brought Gloria Powell along. She's a whiz at reckoning costs and probabilities.'

'I'd like to bet she's a whiz in other directions too,' Carole observed drily.

'There isn't anything like that between her and Jay,' Toni denied awkwardly. 'I thought that once —well, it turns out I was wrong. Jay's told me she's never meant anything to him since we were married, and I believe him.'

'I just hope you're right, honey,' said Carole, rising. 'For myself, I throw a salt mine over my left shoulder where men are concerned.'

'It won't be that way with Jay and me,' Toni offered with the confidence of surety, 'I mean—the way it was between you and your husband. The more I think of it,' she added reflectively, 'the more I realise how young and unrealistic I was then. Jay had certain things to do, goals to reach, and I wanted to fit him into a nine-to-five routine.'

'Let me give you a word of advice, sweetie,'

Carole said with unusual intensity as she stepped closer to Toni. 'A man who neglects his wife in favour of business never changes until it's too late for any woman to care. He'll never go the pipe and slippers route.'

'It's not that way with Jay,' Toni insisted stubbornly. 'He's reached as far as he wants to go, and now——'

'He's ready to settle down?' Carole's shoulders expressed contempt as she went to put a hand on the outer door. 'As I said, honey, I hope you're right, but don't be too disappointed if you find your idol has feet of clay.'

'I'll take my chances.' Toni pushed away the vague feeling of discomfort Carole had aroused. 'Carole, you won't tell anyone about this, will you?'

'About the fact that you're married to the most eligible man in creation? No, honey, I won't. I just hope your sweetly girlish dreams aren't shattered by——' She shrugged. 'Oh, well, we all have to take our chances in the love stakes.'

Toni looked thoughtfully at the door after it had closed behind the other girl. Carole had a jaundiced eye where men were concerned, but that didn't mean that Toni herself had to go along with that thinking. Jay loved her. She knew that now, after a night of blissful lovemaking. No man could pretend the depth of feeling Jay had displayed so ardently, so passionately, unless it was the real thing.

She roused herself and changed quickly into the multi-floral strips of her bikini, covering them with a white boat-necked top and the slacks she had taken from the wardrobe.

She would perform her duties as dedicatedly as always, but this time with the knowledge that her future lay with Jay. No other solution was possible now.

CHAPTER SIX

THE *Aztec Queen* was a dim white silhouette as she nosed her way past the Mexican coastline on her approach to Acapulco. Toni, bright-eyed from the earlier part of the night spent with Jay in his stateroom one deck below, watched from her normal vantage point beneath the bridge as the *Queen* directed her bow round the point encircling the northern perimeter of Acapulco Bay.

Nowhere in the world, she thought admiringly, could have such a stupendous entrance to its harbour. At one moment there was nothing, then suddenly a whole semicircle of pale gold beaches bordered by luxurious high-rise hotels was laid out in a panoramic spread. Tall palms stood sentinel over the quaint thatched huts that provided shade during the hottest part of the day.

To the left as they steamed into harbour, Toni saw again the white-walled villas studded against a brilliant green rise of tropical foliage. The sight never failed to entrance her, and, despite Jay, this morning's arrival was no different from the many others she had known since joining the *Aztec Queen* on her voyages south.

'It's quite something, isn't it?' Jay's voice sounded huskily in her ear, and she was suddenly, potently aware of his lean form pressed intimately to the curved outline of her body.

'I love it,' she responded quietly in deference to

the passengers now crowding the rail. 'Somehow it's always new, unbelievable....'

'How about a second honeymoon here?' he suggested softly. 'We never did have a real honeymoon the first time.'

'No,' she said, her voice strangled in remembrance of the week's honeymoon cut short by Gloria's call back to business. 'I'd prefer Puerto Vallarta, I think, for something as special as that.'

'Whatever you say,' he agreed in a docile way, though there was nothing passive about the male hardness of his body pressed to hers. It was worth all the knowing glances from the crew, she decided happily as the wind lifted her hair. Pearson had spread the word like wildfire through the ship, but she had detected no ill will in the smiles sent in her direction.

Except maybe for Rick Warren, whose grimace of distaste could hardly be described as a smile. 'You'll find the money correct, I believe,' he had said coldly the day before when handing over the cash float for the Acapulco tours. Before Toni had had a chance to do more than murmur her thanks, he had turned away from her and walked into the inner office.

It was too bad about Rick, but she couldn't remain dull at his memory when the glittering spectacle of Acapulco lay before her as if spread out for her own delight. The rising sun glinted whitely off the high-rise hotels to her right, and cast a sideways shadow over the coconut palms.

'Do you have to babysit bus passengers today?' Jay murmured.

'No.' Toni's heart was in her eyes when she threw him a quick backward smile. 'We're always free in Acapulco, and I thought you could rent a car to take us to a very quiet, very private beach I know.'

'You're very free with my time and money, aren't you?' he growled against her hair.

'Well, certainly,' she laughed, 'after all, you're——'

'Jay, I've been looking everywhere for you!'

Gloria's voice came from behind them and they both turned to see the early morning tightness on her pale face. She was dressed in a midi-blouse of tangerine cotton, a colour that did nothing to help her skin, and white hip-hugging jeans.

'Oh?'

Jay detached himself casually from Toni and gave his full attention to the other girl. Irritation rose up like a wave inside her.

'This radio message came in overnight, it seems.' Gloria's flat blue eyes flickered momentarily over Toni. 'Naturally, when you couldn't be reached in your stateroom, it was brought to me. As you'll see, it appears urgent that you return to Los Angeles immediately. I've already checked on planes, and there's one you can take out of Acapulco at ten-thirty this morning.'

Jay read the scrap of paper with a deeply etched frown between his dark brows. 'Damn,' he swore softly. 'Why can't Ansell wait until I get back?'

'It's an important contract, Jay,' Gloria returned smoothly, ignoring Toni now. 'And you know how particular Jacob Ansell is. He wouldn't want to talk with anyone but the principal in something as big as this.'

Jay swore again under his breath, and seemed to have forgotten Toni too in his spate of instructions to the efficient Gloria. As he spoke, they moved across the deck out of earshot of the other passengers—and Toni.

She turned back to the rail, but the magnificent bay showed up as a wavering mirage through her tear-filled eyes. Nothing had changed, not one thing. There would always be just one more deal for Jay. Why had she been so foolish as to think he had meant what he said about being a supervisory figurehead? It was in his nature to be that kind of man. Heaven knew he must have enough money to live in idle luxury for the rest of his life, but that wasn't what drove him.

The tears had been blinked away and her surface composure was in place when he came back to slide his arms round her again.

'I'm sorry, sweetheart, but I have to take off for a while. I'd arranged this meeting for after the cruise, but it seems Ansell is in two minds whether to take my offer or someone else's.' He turned her in his arms, then drew her away from the rail. His eyes were sombre, yet they were lit far back with tiny sparks.

'I want you to come with me, Toni. We can fly back to join the ship at Puerto Vallarta.'

'Me?' She stared up into his lean face. 'That's impossible. I work here, remember?'

'You did work here,' he corrected, smiling. 'Now

you're Mrs Jay Stanford again, and I want you with me at all times.'

'I thought you did, too,' she said sadly, pulling out of his arms and stepping round him. 'But I see now I was mistaken. You'll never change, Jay.'

'What in hell are you talking about?' He caught her arm and turned her forcibly to face him, his jaw firmed to white anger. I told you about this last deal, and I want you with me when I clinch it.'

'The last deal,' she mocked, ignoring the bruising hurt of his fingers as they gouged her flesh. 'There's never going to be a last deal for you, Jay. You don't need the money, but you'll go on ruining our lives to get it.'

'Whatever else I've done,' he gritted, 'I've never lied to you. This deal with Ansell is the last, and *I want you with me when I make it!*'

'Take Gloria,' she flashed, and tore herself from his grasp.

'Maybe I'll do just that,' he called after her fleeing figure in a voice of steel.

But he didn't. Toni didn't know or care if the blonde woman had joined him as usual on his business flight from Acapulco, so she was only mildly surprised when Gloria sought her out in her below decks cabin. The white evening dress Toni had forgotten to remove from Jay's stateroom was folded over her arm, and she breezed past Toni when the door was opened to her peremptory knock.

'I thought you might need this,' she said loftily, raising carefully darkened brows in a derogatory arc as she glanced round the confined space. 'Do two of you actually live here?'

Toni, annoyed by her own forgetfulness in retrieving the dress, snapped irritably: 'We find it adequate.'

Gloria deposited the dress on Carole's berth and cast another glance around the small room before resting her pale blue eyes on Toni again.

'Adequate—that's always been your problem, you know. You're content with an adequate life, an adequate husband. Neither of which Jay could give you.'

'You're such an expert on human relationships?' Toni scorned, wedging herself against the door she had just closed. The two ship's nurses shared a cabin directly opposite, and one of them was always off duty.

'I'm an expert on Jay Stanford,' Gloria stated coolly. She settled her narrow hips on Toni's neatly made berth. 'You've never known how to cope with a man like him, have you?'

Toni gave her a level look. 'I've been managing pretty well lately,' she said with pointed sarcasm.

'You really are gullible, aren't you?' Gloria's knowing smile was more of a sneer, and Toni's self-assurance dropped a few notches in face of the other girl's confident air.

'I—don't know what you mean.'

'It's very simple, sweetie, once you know the details.' Gloria's blonde features settled into hardness. 'You were so anxious to hop back into bed with him that you didn't question his motives at all, did you?' She laughed harshly. 'Why do you think Jay suddenly made a point of seeking you out? Because he was madly in love with the naïve little idiot you always were?'

Knees that shook with sudden tremors propelled Toni to the hard-backed chair near the bathroom entrance. What Gloria was saying, implying, was prompted by jealousy. A jealousy that had dated from Jay's first announcement of their engagement. Yet....

'Jay and I love each other in a way you couldn't begin to understand,' she began, her mouth firming when Gloria again laughed derisively.

'Jay doesn't know the meaning of your sickening kind of love,' she jeered. 'He happened to need you at this particular time, and you fell for his line of undying devotion. Believe me, sweetie, he needed you in the worst way, but not for the reason you think.'

'And I suppose you know the reason?'

'Certainly I do. Jay and I have been together since long before you ever laid eyes on him, and I know which drummer he marches to.' Gloria crossed her slender legs and went on conversationally: 'This deal he's involved with now is the biggest one of his career. It could make him rich beyond your girlish dreams.'

Genuine bewilderment clouded Toni's eyes. The other woman's insinuation that she had married Jay because of his financial standing wasn't worth the trouble of denying. It was the sureness in Gloria's manner that made her heartbeat race erratically.

'What does the deal have to do with me?'

'It has everything to do with you,' Gloria stated

dramatically, rising and taking a pace or two away from the berth, a frown of irritation creasing her brow when she came up short against the dresser. 'Jacob Ansell is a very powerful man, with a lot of fingers in different pies. He's also a very religious man, and he disapproves strongly of divorce, even separation between married couples. To get the contract, Jay has to produce a loving wife with no thoughts in her starry eyes of separation, let alone divorce.'

'I don't believe you!' Toni suppressed the quiver in her voice, knowing as she denied them that the words had a ring of truth about them. Jay had apparently functioned very well for the two years of their separation, had even filed for divorce although he had changed his mind later. Had the prospective deal with Jacob Ansell come up at that time and made it more effective policy to patch up their storm-swept marriage? One thing was sure. Jay had lost no time after coming aboard in weaving his magic spell around her senses, the familiar spell he knew she was powerless to resist.

'Don't you? I think you do, honey.' Gloria crossed to the door and curved her hand round the knob. 'Didn't Jay ask you to go with him to L.A.?' She laughed at the stricken look in Toni's eyes. 'You see, I understand him a lot better than you ever will.'

Toni mustered a final defiant: 'It hasn't got you very far, has it?'

Gloria smiled tautly. 'Hasn't it? You're just too sweetly innocent for words! Jay's realised for some time now that you're far from being the wife he needs.'

The door opened suddenly on a hard inner
thrust, and Carole stared with startled eyes into the
pale orbs that matched her own.

'Oh. Am I interrupting something?'

'Not at all,' Gloria answered breezily, stepping
out into the narrow corridor. 'Your friend might
need a little reinforcing, though.'

Carole closed the door on Gloria's retreating
figure and stared questioningly at Toni. 'What was
all that about?'

Toni shrugged and got up from the chair, going
moodily to the dressing table and staring sightlessly
at her own reflection in the mirror.

'She's a number one bitch,' she bit off with unusual savagery, and saw Carole's immediate shrug
in her mirrored reflection.

'I could have told you that from the start,' she
said in her cool, collected way. 'What brought her
slumming this morning?'

Needing a sympathetic audience, Toni let the
words trip from her tongue, and when she had exhausted the supply Carole looked with commisera-
tion at her.

'I won't say I'm not sorry for you, Toni, but
you've really been a first class dope in this occasion.
I'm inclined to agree with our fine feathered friend
that your Jay has been using you for his own ends.
Why else would he suddenly put in an appearance
on this old tub? Let's be honest. No business man
in his right mind would take on such a losing proposition unless he had some other motive.' Carole gave
her a shrewd glance. 'Has he actually said he'd put
up cold hard cash for the *Queen*?'

'No,' Toni admitted reluctantly. 'He knows how much it means to—to all of us, and he's thinking about it.'

'Believe me, honey, that's as far as he'll go!' Carole exclaimed impatiently as she put a bracing hand on Toni's shoulder. 'Men are the pits sometimes—most of the time, in my experience. Why don't you try putting him out of your mind? Heaven forbid I should recommend the Purser, but he'd never have that kind of power to hurt you.'

Toni gave a wan smile. 'Communications between Rick and me are definitely closed. After Jay, he's—well, I think Marian's better for him than I could ever be.'

'Marian?' Carole stared at her incredulously. 'I know she has an outsize crush on the man, but— *Marian?*'

'With a different hairdo and a little help with her make-up, I think she'd be just fine for Rick,' Toni defended. 'In fact, I've suggested a trip to the beauty salon and offered to give her a few pointers on cosmetics. She didn't take too well to the idea, though, and I haven't heard from her since,' she ended abstractedly.

'That's not surprising, considering it's you she hopes to replace in our estimable Purser's eyes,' Carole quipped drily. 'Look, honey, forget about Rick Warren, Marian, and your not so ex-husband. And the quickest way to do that is to find somebody else.' She added casually as she opened a drawer to rummage through its contents: 'Who was the man I saw you with that night you made a foursome at dinner?'

Toni stared blankly for a moment before comprehension dawned. 'Oh, you mean Cyrus Jackson? You're suggesting that I——? For heaven's sake, Carole, he's more than old enough to be my father!'

'What does that have to do with anything?' Closing the drawer with a satisfied grunt, Carole fastened a white shell necklace round her throat and looked contemplatively at its effect in the mirror. 'He's unattached, and he seemed attracted to you.'

An irrepressible giggle rose from Toni. 'I'd feel he was my daddy taking me out for a special treat! Besides,' she sobered, 'I like Cyrus. He never took time out to be married—like Jay, he's devoted his life to the making of money.'

'All to the better that you like him. I'm not saying you should take him on as a permanent thing, but a little flirtation won't do either of you any harm. In fact,' Carole's blue eyes took on a thoughtful look, 'it could settle things one way or the other for you. Is this husband of yours planning on joining the ship again before we get back to L.A.?'

Toni shrugged. 'He said something about Puerto Vallarta.'

'Then a little competition might smarten up his ideas. This Cyrus Jackson is a very different kettle of fish from our starchy Purser!' Carole picked up a white bag to match the accessories on her aqua dress. 'Anyway, think about it, Toni. I'm going to show Mike around Acapulco, and we're taking the bus tour out to the Princess Hotel tonight. Why don't you come?'

'I thought I should go with the group to watch

the cliff diving at the El Mirador,' Toni said doubtfully.

'It's not necessary for you to do that,' Carole returned crisply from the door. 'We're entitled to the
time off in Acapulco.' She opened the door and
stepped into the passage. 'Think about it, and I'll
check with you later.'

Toni spent the remainder of the daylight hours on
board, disinclined to wander amongst the fun-
seeking tourists occupying the beaches and hotel
bars ashore. She hadn't realised, until now, how
much she had been looking forward to showing Jay
the sights of this most cosmopolitan centre on the
Mexican Riviera. They could have rented a car, as
she had seen Cyrus Jackson and Gloria do, and seen
all the sights independently, finishing off with a
swim further along the coast.

But she might as well put thoughts like those out
of her mind permanently, she reminded herself
firmly as she checked supplies for the masquerade
party to be held just after the ship left Puerto
Vallarta.

Jay's perfidy had once more left her out on an emotional limb, and she was determined it would be the
last time. The unhappiness that was a solid ball of
hurt in her middle would take a long time to melt
to the point where the hurt would be less, but she
had done it before and she could do it again. Maybe
Carole was right, and flitting from man to man
was preferable to the ups and downs of a permanent relationship. At least that way the pain, if any,
was transitory.

Her mind was far from the flat rolls of crêpe paper in varied colours which she sorted through in the wall cupboards behind the Entertainment Desk in the main lobby when Marian said diffidently behind her:

'Are you busy, Toni?'

Toni swung round to stare at the other girl's puckered brow and nervous hand-wringing.

'Not really,' she said with a short laugh. 'Just filling in time until I can go and change for dinner.'

'Oh, that's good. I mean,' Marian added hastily, 'I wanted to talk to you, but I didn't want to bother you if you were busy. It's not exactly about ship's business,' she ended lamely.

'Go ahead.' Toni leaned back against the cupboards and contemplated her curiously, noting the white uniform dress as immaculate as always, and the tidy, if not imaginative, style of her hair. If only, she sighed inwardly. . . .

'It's just that—well, I've been thinking about what you said the other day, and I—I think I'd like to try the new look you suggested.'

Toni emerged sharply from her own misery. 'Oh, sure. I'd be glad to do anything I can to help. Not with your hair—Donna's the one for that—but I'll help you choose some cosmetics and show you how to use them.'

'Thanks.' Marian sought awkwardly for words of appreciation. 'It's good of you to——'

'My pleasure,' Toni interrupted lightly, scanning the other girl's face with an impartial eye. 'I think the shop on board can supply all we need, but the beauty salon won't be open until we sail.'

Marian said quickly: 'That's fine. I thought I'd
—wait until the day of the masquerade party, then
it wouldn't seem such a big deal to—people.'

'People' meaning Rick, Toni reflected wryly, but
it was good thinking on Marian's part. In the general
gaiety and excitement of the costume party, a dras-
tic alteration in her appearance would be less notice-
able than if she just turned up that way behind the
Purser's deck one morning.

Glad to push away her own morose thoughts, she
initiated a discussion on the costume Marian was
intending to wear, contrary to her normal practice
of appearing by the Captain's side in starched uniform.

'I thought I might come up with an idea between
now and then,' she confessed shyly. 'As you know,
I've never bothered before, but I'd like to be—
totally different this time.'

Toni skimmed mentally through her own standing wardrobe of masquerade costumes. The Cleopatra outfit would do nothing for Marian—besides,
she had planned to wear that herself this time
around—but the flapper dress, complete with head-
band and elongated cigarette holder, would be perfect for her. It was one she herself hadn't worn often,
so not even Rick would recognise it on such a totally different personality's as Marian's.

Her own enthusiasm rubbed off on the assistant
purser, and Marian's cheeks had taken on a faint,
unaccustomed glow when two early returnees from
the day's sightseeing emerged into the hall from
the rope-enclosed stairway from the dock below.

'Thank God for modern technology,' Gloria

Powell threw out irritably as she took in a deep breath of the air-conditioned atmosphere. 'How do people survive in that kind of heat?'

'Maybe they're used to it,' Cyrus offered to her perspiring back, his own face a mottled red of discomfort.

'Well, I'm not,' she snapped pettishly, and dragged herself off towards the elevators without a backward glance or word of thanks to her daytime escort.

Cyrus leaned against the counter where Toni and Marian faced each other, mopping his brow as he said ruefully: 'Some women just can't take the heat. I'm not sure I can, either.'

'It takes some getting used to,' Toni agreed, smiling. Belatedly remembering her manners, she introduced him to Marian.

'I'd better get back,' the latter murmured as a shorts-clad woman came from one of the passages and leaned enquiringly on the Purser's counter. Cyrus looked after her quizzically.

'There's a girl who needs a little of your spark and personality,' he observed shrewdly.

'Wait a while,' advised Toni, her eyes taking on a determined glow. 'You just might be surprised come masquerade night.'

'Why? Does she cast off her inhibitions then?' Cyrus queried with a blue-eyed twinkle. 'The werewolf lady of the *Aztec Queen*?'

'No,' Toni laughed in return, 'but she might cause quite a stir this time, if I have my way.'

Cyrus gave her a piercing look. 'I imagine you do get your own way as far as men are concerned, anyway.' He added casually: 'I hear our James Brownlea has deserted the ship.'

Toni busied her hands beneath the counter top in an imaginary shuffling of papers. 'Yes. Temporarily, anyway.'

'What happened? Did his wife find out where he was and send out the royal summons?'

'I don't believe so. He had some business to attend to in Los Angeles.'

A faint glint of compassion lit Cyrus's eyes as they met hers above the counter. 'Don't hold that against him,' he said softly. 'A man has certain things he has to do in this life.'

'So I understand,' Toni returned more coolly than she had intended.

After a slight pause, he asked: 'Would you happen to be free this evening?'

Toni blinked, surprised by his question. 'Aren't you taking Gloria around the Acapulco night spots?' She would have thought the blonde girl would enjoy seeing how the beautiful people celebrated night life in the cosmopolitan resort.

'I doubt it,' he chuckled, seeming more amused than hurt. 'I don't have your ex-boss's abilities in the man-about-town department. She'd been planning great things for them at this particular spot, which as you must know would be pretty exciting with the right person.'

A stab of hurt pierced Toni's middle. 'Yes,' she agreed quietly, 'I guess it would.' As a counter-reaction, she forced a smile to her lips. 'As a matter of fact Carole, the Cruise Director, asked if I'd like to join her and a friend at the Princess Hotel tonight. I don't know if you'd care to——?'

'I'd be honoured,' Cyrus beamed with jovial
courtesy, and Toni, liking him very much at that
moment, outlined the details of the evening bus
tour. 'Can't we have dinner together somewhere
first?'

'The bus leaves at nine,' Toni said regretfully,
'and I'm afraid the dinner hour in Acapulco is quite
a bit later than that.'

'Well, then you'd better join me in the dining
room here at seven-fifteen,' he said firmly. 'My table
is number twenty-three.'

Deciding that the dining room would be more
than half empty and that no one would be likely to
object to a mingling of passengers and crew—even
the Captain kept himself to himself in port—Toni
nodded her acquiescence and watched Cyrus'
jaunty walk as he passed through the hall.

He was a nice man, and if it gave an extra fillip
to his vacation to take a much younger woman out
for the evening, so much the better.

A few minutes later, after locking the cupboards
she had been checking through, she stopped for a
word with Marian on her way below. There was an
unmistakably envious look about the other girl's
face.

'How do you do it?' she blurted out, reddening as
she realised how rude the words sounded. 'I mean,
you've got Rick on a string, and Mr Brownlea, and
now when he's not available, somebody elese turns
up.'

Rapidly rejecting a flip answer, Toni regarded
Marian seriously. 'Rick hates the ground I walk on

right now, Mr Brownlea can live very happily without me, and Cyrus Jackson is happily married to his financial empire—not to mention that he's old enough to be my father. If you want to know the truth, I envy you because you have no doubts about which man you're in love with and want to share your life with.'

Marian gaped at her with astonished eyes. '*You* envy *me*?' she repeated, shocked.

'And I'll envy you even more when Rick opens his eyes and sees you as the woman of his dreams,' Toni ended on a light note as she walked from the Purser's desk and made her way to the elevator.

If she had been keeping a box score, she reflected wryly, she could chalk up two successes against one dismal failure. Marian's confidence had increased significantly lately, and would reach a peak by her groomed appearance on the night of the masquerade party. Cyrus Jackson had been given a lift, if only temporary, by the prospect of an evening's fun spent in the company of young people.

The only sour note came in her own relationship to Jay. Why, oh, why had she fallen in love with a man who, like Cyrus, was already married to the world of big business where personal relationships took a back seat.

Golf courses stretched out from left to right as the tour bus traversed the wide drive leading to the Acapulco Princess Hotel.

The impressive pyramidal structure itself was surrounded by tropical gardens studded, in floodlit splendour, by the bright flame colour of poinsettias growing uninhibitedly on shrub-sized plants. Toni, pulling her black silk stole closer around her shoulders as they walked the last few steps to the hotel foyer, thought wryly about her mother's long-ago attempts to coax colour into the green bracts of the small house plants she had cherished.

'Oh, boy,' Cyrus murmured as they entered the vast hotel foyer, 'isn't this something?'

The note of awe in his voice echoed the feeling Toni always had on entering the massive hall where live trees and shrubs thrived despite the soaring structure around them, Looking up, she saw galleried hotel floors ascending in ever narrowing tiers to the penthouse at its pinnacle.

The lobby was crowded with hotel residents and those who, like themselves, had come to spend the evening in one of the many lounges, bars and dining rooms.

Carole, in her best Cruise Director manner, shepherded their group to the spacious lounge toward the rear, speaking to the management representative in fluent Spanish before beckoning to Toni and the two men.

They were led to a table edging the dance floor, and almost before they were seated, the first two free drinks supplied for the tour customers was placed in front of them by an attentive waiter.

'Well,' Cyrus leaned back expansively in his chair opposite Carole's, 'this promises to be a great evening's entertainment.'

His words proved prophetic, and even Toni managed to push thoughts of Jay to the back of her mind as Mexican dancers in colourful costumes entertained them. The dramatic and comic routines leapt the language barrier and left the audience in tears of laughter.

Mike's slow but steady good humour was a perfect foil for Cyrus's ready wit, and their table was the liveliest around the dance floor.

Toni decided that she liked Mike very much, his attitude towards Carole being just what, in her opinion, the other girl badly needed. He was solid, attentive without being overwhelming, and with just the right touch of humour to lighten his solemnity.

Later, when the show was over and dancing had begun, Toni found herself lodged comfortably in his arms as they moved in a slow glide between the other dancers.

'This cruise is going to end far too soon for me,' he smiled into her eyes. 'Strange, when I didn't want to come on it in the first place.'

'So why did you?' Toni asked curiously.

He shrugged. 'My boss had been on one with his wife, and he thought it would be a good idea. We'd been working pretty hard, so he arranged it all for me—expenses paid.'

'He must think a lot of you,' Toni smiled back. 'What do you do, exactly?'

'Nothing exciting. In fact, most people would be bored to death with my job. I'm an accountant,' he ended on a grin.

'Oh. That's not a bit dull to lots of business people, you know. They'd be lost without their accounts experts.'

Mike's warm brown eyes clouded. 'Maybe so, but

most women look on accountants as people who are as dry as the figures they deal with.' There was an imperceptible pause before he went on casually: 'I guess you and Carole meet a lot of interesting people on these cruises. Like the James Brownlea who might be buying the ship. His kind must have a lot of appeal for women.'

Toni gave her absent cabin-mate first prize for discretion regarding her own relationship to Jay, but marked her low in showing her obvious enthusiasm for men of Jay's calibre.

'For some women, maybe,' she lifted her shoulders slightly, 'but Carole's never struck me as a girl impressed too much by wealth or standing. She's—' she searched for the right phrase—'Carole's more impressed by a man's personal worth, I would say, than in how his bank balance rises.'

Mike nodded thoughtfully, steering her through the couples dancing in a more abandoned fashion around the edges of the floor. 'She's had a bad time where men are concerned.'

'That's why she needs somebody who's—solid, dependable,' Toni returned soberly. 'With the right person, she'd be able to forget——' She left the remainder of the sentence in the air, knowing Mike could fill in the blank for himself.

The drink awaiting them at the table was Toni's fourth, and after drinking it she felt detached from her surroundings, detached from her feelings about Jay.

Loving him, he had made use of that love in his businesslike way. So what? She had managed to exist for two years without him, and she could do it for a lifetime if necessary.

Dimly she heard Cyrus say something about a taxi, Carole's faint murmur, then found herself in the back seat of a car that sped quickly through the dark night.

The ship at dockside was ablaze with lights, unreal somehow as Toni stumbled up the swaying steps, a man's hands firm at her waist propelling her upward....

CHAPTER SEVEN

THE ship was already under way when Toni opened her eyes the following morning. Her head throbbed in unison with the engines not far below, and her throat raged with an unfamiliar thirst.

Her agonised groan brought a startlingly neat Carole to look commiseratingly down at her.

'I—I think I'm seasick,' she moaned.

'And I think you have a hangover,' Carole retorted briskly, though her eyes were not unkind as they looked down into Toni's. 'Here, take these.' She proffered two aspirins on the palm of her hand and thrust a paper cup of water towards Toni. 'Don't worry about the exercise session, I've already done it.'

Toni stared at her dazedly, her hair a black contrast to the whiteness of her pillow. 'You've already——? What time is it?'

'Eight-thirty. Go back to sleep now. I'll organise the deck tennis tournament, and you can do the afternoon bingo game.'

Had she muttered her thanks as Carole left the cabin? Toni swallowed the aspirins and sank back into a deep sleep of oblivion until she reluctantly opened her eyes to the starkly accusing bedside clock whose hands stood at eleven-thirty.

Half an hour later, showered and dressed in white pleated skirt and sleeveless top, she stood on the

Promenade Deck gulping deep lungfuls of sea air, feeling better yet worse by the minute.

What had possessed her to make her abandon her long-standing dislike of too much strong liquor, for herself or anyone else? And what must Cyrus Jackson think of her? Somehow that was very important to her. He was nice, kind, like the father she had lost by fire in Seattle.

'Does some soup and a sandwich appeal to you?'

Toni turned to see Cyrus's amused yet kindly face not far from her shoulder. 'Not really,' she said faintly.

'Still,' he took a firm hold on her bare elbow, 'I think you should put something in your stomach. There's a deck buffet today, so you won't be stuck in the enclosed atmosphere of the dining room. I already have a table on the other side—what's it called, starboard?'

'Port,' Toni summoned up weakly, and she was glad of his firm support as they crossed from one side of the deck to the other. Truth to tell, her stomach *was* beginning to feel empty, since she had eaten nothing since their dinner together the evening before.

Cyrus demanded nothing of her, disappearing after seating her at the railside table covered by a gay red and white checked cloth and coming back a short time later with beef *bouillon* in a cup, and thinly sliced ham between innocuous white bread slices.

'What about you?' she asked when he took the seat opposite and seemed prepared to watch her eat.

'I've already eaten. Sea air certainly sharpens the

appetite,' he glanced down wryly at his generous frame. 'I think I'd better steer clear of cruises in future.'

'Just like you've steered clear of wives?' Toni asked between sips of the appetising clear broth.

'And wives,' he agreed gravely, his eyes softly knowing as he looked at her across the table. 'That's something you know quite a lot about, I guess.'

'Me?' Toni finished the last of the dark brown liquid and carefully set the cup aside. 'I've been married, of course, everybody knows that. But my husband isn't—wasn't—the kind of man who took kindly to wifely pampering.'

'But I gathered last night that pampering him is still what you'd like to do.'

Toni's head snapped up in a defensive—and painful—arc. 'So? I was brought up that way. The only thing wrong with my teaching was that my husband didn't find it necessary to his happiness. My mother didn't prepare me for that.'

'All men want to be pampered,' Cyrus said gently. 'Even your Jay Stanford.'

Her lips parted in a *moue* of disbelief as she stared across the table at him, her fingers as white as the bread they held. 'I don't know what you're talking about,' she said finally, replacing the sandwich on the plate before her.

Cyrus looked at her consideringly. 'Last night,' he said slowly, 'you told me that Jay Stanford was your husband, and that you still care for him an awful lot. I've heard the scuttlebut going around about you and James Brownlea getting cosy in his stateroom, and—well, you don't strike me as the kind of girl who sleeps around, even with the pro-spective buyer of the *Aztec Queen*. It occurred to me,' he finished on a lighter tone, 'that Jay Stanford and James Brownlea might be one and the same person.'

Although no food had passed her lips, Toni felt a hard constriction in her throat. She'd been more indiscreet than she had imagined last night, the worst of it being that she couldn't remember men-tioning Jay the whole evening.

But what did that matter? It was over between her and Jay, and it really didn't matter if the whole world knew of their relationship.

She swallowed hard. 'Yes, they're one and the same person.' Slowly, hesitatingly, she explained the whole situation to Cyrus, who listened alertly though saying nothing. 'So,' she ended on a bitter note, 'there never was a James Brownlea aboard, and there never was a possibility of Jay buying the *Queen*. It was all a put-up job to give Jay a lever over me. He used me for his own ends.' Indignant tears made her dark eyes glint.

Cyrus reached a comforting hand across the table to cover hers. 'Aren't you condemning him out of hand?' he suggested mildly, then went on conversa-tionally, giving her time to recover her composure: 'You know, when I was quite a lot younger there was a girl I was really in love with, and I believed she was with me. We made plans to be married many times, but something always came up in my business world to postpone the wedding. When I finally de-cided I could take the time off to squeeze in a honey-moon, she told me she was marrying another man who loved her more than his accountant's balance sheet.' He smiled wryly. 'I know you're going to say she was right, but—well, I still think we could have had a good life together.'

Toni swallowed a different kind of lump in her throat. 'I'm sorry, Cyrus. Do you—still see her?'

He shook his greying head and said painfully: 'She died a couple of years ago. We met from time to time over the years, and I think she was happy with her life—or at least content. One of her three sons is up and coming in my company.'

'I'm sorry,' she said again.

'Don't be. Just don't let Jay make the same mistake I did. He's still young enough to do something about it.'

'Maybe you should be telling him that, not me.'

'Maybe I will,' he shrugged, 'if he ever comes back on board.'

The question of whether or not Jay would return from Los Angeles was one that plagued Toni for the remainder of the sea miles before they reached Puerto Vallarta.

Part of her shied away from the inevitable confrontation between them, but mostly she gave in to the deep-seated longing to see his lithely fit figure striding the decks again, to feel the hard urgency of his body commanding hers, to hear the husky murmur of his voice at her ear.

But Puerto Vallarta came and went without sight or sound of him.

Going ashore by launch to the romantic Spanish-type port, she tried to put Jay from her mind. The tour bus guide, one she was familiar with, greeted her warmly. His name, Jésus, was one he made great play on with the tourists.

'What better hands could you be in?' he would ask tongue in cheek, small and handsome in white short-sleeved shirt and beige drill slacks. Still, he was a fount of information on the past and recent history of the town, and of the Mexican political scene so close to his heart.

A Mass was about to be said at the Church of Our Lady of Guadeloupe close to the main plaza, so the tourist groups were given only a cursory tour of the ornately decorated chapel with its backdrop of Mexico's red, green and white national colours.

Outside, two small girls obviously on their way to confirmation shyly commanded a large audience of tourists intent on filming them in their long white lace dresses that made them look like miniature brides. Smiling, Toni shepherded her own group back to the plaza, which was lined with colonial buildings used as offices for the town's officials. Ahead was the sea, an incredible mixture of blue and turquoise.

Installed again in the bus, they were given a glimpse of Puerto Vallarta's Spanish red-tiled roofs before driving along the coastline past the sea-front estates of the wealthy and luxury hotels boasting white sand beaches.

'Look, there's the ship,' one woman cried when they stopped at the cliff edge to look back on the town and wide bay.

The *Aztec Queen* was, indeed, anchored in the bay, looking trim and white and far from her real age. That thought sponsored another in Toni. Had Jay ever thought seriously of buying her and giving her a new lease of life? If only he could see her from this angle! To anyone with an eye for ships, she was truly beautiful.

But, Toni sighed as she turned away, Jay had no eyes to spare for the romance of a ship plying the trade she was built for. To him, she was just a profit and loss balance on an audit sheet.

Back in town, Toni made her own way back to the ship, leaving the passengers browsing happily in the gift stores and flea market where bargains abounded. The quayside, too, was a thriving bustle of stalls selling everything from hand-embroidered dresses to cheap and cheerful jewellery. On the launch, passengers vied with one another to see who had made the best bargain in the straw bags and trinkets they clutched contentedly.

The ship's air-conditioning struck pleasantly cool after the humid shore heat, and Toni decided to take a cold drink on deck and watch the returning passengers. Eddy, the barman, obliged with his own recipe of lemon, lime, vodka, and ice that tinkled pleasantly against her glass as she stepped out on deck again.

Constantly plying launches were returning with ever greater loads as the afternoon progressed. Toni's eyes scanned each one of them quickly, looking for yet dreading to see Jay's casually commanding presence dominating the bargain-happy passengers.

The last boat had been winched up to the Boat Deck and night, which fell so quickly in Mexico, was bringing out a string of lights ashore when she turned away from the rail, the empty glass in her hand, a pale figure loomed out of the surrounding dimness and said hesitantly:

'Toni?'

For a moment, Toni stared without recognition at a transformed Marian. The trim white uniform dress was the same, but the face above it had taken on a rounded fullness, a cherub-like impishness from the short curls rioting round her head.

'Marian?'

The normally staid girl was shy as she asked: 'Do you like it?'

Toni let out a long-held lungful of breath. 'It's— fantastic! You look great! Donna's an absolute genius!'

Marian's beaming smile came and went on uncertainly. 'You don't think it's too much of a change?'

'It's a big change,' admitted Toni consideringly, 'but nobody in his right mind would object to it.'

They both knew that she was referring to Rick's possible reaction to his assistant's transformation into an attractive girl who suddenly looked years younger than her normal appearance suggested.

'I wondered if you'd have the time to help me with the make-up for my costume later.' Marian hesitated again. 'But I guess you'll be busy with your own.'

'I'll be glad to. I've worn the Cleopatra costume so many times I could get ready with my eyes shut. Toni took the other girl's arm, glad to shelve her own thoughts. 'Let's go and make you into a fun-loving flapper!'

*

Strains of music drifted out from the main lounge as Toni hurried up to the Crowsnest Club later that evening. All the participants in the Grand Masquerade Parade would be gathered there, waiting to descend to the main lounge *en masse* for their appearance before the audience not inclined to participate themselves.

There was always a nucleus of fun-loving, imaginatively creative passengers who made this evening a success, Toni reflected as she looked round the laughing, chattering groups of Harlequins, Robin Hoods complete with their Maid Marians, clowns and elder statesmen. Carole, a bewigged Madame Pompadour, seemed relieved to see Toni.

'You're late,' she said crisply from behind a plain brown table where she was dispensing entry numbers to be pinned on to the participants' costumes.

'Sorry, I had to help Marian with her outfit.'

Toni slid behind the table, and smiled to a mature woman dressed as an infant.

'Marian?' Carole asked blankly.

Toni wrote down the pseudo-baby's name and cabin number, pinning the white paper with black numbering to a voluminous diaper.

'She looks sensational,' she turned back to Carole, referring to Marian.

Carole's brows lifted. 'Really?' she gave a sarcastic drawl. 'That must have taken some doing.'

'No, really, she does,' Toni said absently, pondering as to just where she should pin the entry card on a scantily clad Eve.

'Evidently the one she hopes to impress hasn't seen her yet,' Carole observed drily, looking towards the entrance where Captain Vance and Rick

Warren had put in an appearance. 'He looks as morose as always.'

Captain Vance usually timed his arrival for when most of the participants had been processed and were relaxing over complimentary cocktails before descending to the waiting audience below. An aura of excited anticipation filled the room as it must, Toni had often thought, backstage before the beginning of a stage performance.

The Captain, staunchly erect in his tropical whites, lifted a beckoning hand in her direction, and she gave Carole an apologetic smile before gliding over to where Captain Vance and Rick stood. Gliding was all she could do in the glittering gold lamé dress which followed closely the curves and indentations of her figure. Cleopatra had obviously never accompanied Antony on his marches!

'You look exotic as always in your Nile get-up,' the Captain told her gruffly, alert eyes under beetling grey brows roving over the thick black lines around her eyes, the heavy gold medallion resting above the cleft formed by her confined breasts. Turning to Rick, who was studiously avoiding Toni's appealing gaze, he added abruptly: 'Okay, go and circulate. Tell them all how great they look.'

His eyes took on a softer expression as they rested on Toni again. 'You must be busier than usual this trip. I don't seem to have seen so much of you.'

'There does seem to have been a lot to do, sir,' Toni returned, far from feeling as glib as she sounded. It was inevitable that the Captain, although he might be the last to hear it, was the recipient of all the ship's gossip.

'Well, don't overdo the devotion to duty routine,'

he said heavily. 'Remember, your father was my good friend, and I'm interested in your welfare.' Seeming to change the subject, though in reality homing in closer to the point of his conversation, he asked casually: 'Have you seen anything of James Brownlea lately?'

'I believe he went to L.A. on business, sir.'

'True, but I understood he'd be joining us again at Puerto Vallarta.'

'He may have, Captain, I haven't seen him.'

Hyram Vance nodded thoughtfully, then turned to leave the lounge, his duty done, looking back over his shoulder to say: 'Don't feel you have to go beyond your own inclinations where the ship's concerned. Like all of us, she has to go to the graveyard one day.'

He left Toni with that cryptic message, then escaped from the lounge. She knew he was more comfortable on the bridge or in his quarters than in exerting himself socially with the passengers. Her own brow was furrowed in thought as she went slowly back to Carole's side. Should she have told the Captain that there had never been the remotest possibility of Jay's buying the ship?

Deciding to let sleeping dogs lie, she looked around at the assembled contestants. They were all mustered now, and in just a few minutes they would start to wend their way below for the highlight of the evening before dancing to the ship's orchestra began.

The costume parade was over, the prizes awarded, and now the floor was filled with oddly assorted couples. Beast danced with Beauty, Lincoln with Nell Gwynn, Hansel with Gretel. Almost everyone entering the contest was awarded a prize of some sort in the various categories, and good spirits reigned in the spacious lounge.

Toni, from her stance just inside the entrance, felt like a den mother pleased with the efforts of her charges. Many of the masqueraders would not be cavorting around the floor now had it not been for her persuasive cajolery. Some of those who had resisted her blandishments had looked faintly wistful during the parade, as if they regretted not making the effort to join in the fun.

Gloria had disdained a costume, and sat with an expression of acute boredom on her alabaster features throughout the ceremonies, her severe long black dress emphasising her creamy shoulders and fashionably styled blonde hair.

Cyrus, an authentic-looking Friar Tuck in brown habit tied with a white rope belt, had taken the seat beside her and had evidently given up on conversation with her, his eyes roaming restlessly over the dancing couples.

Could a nice man like Cyrus Jackson be seriously interested in a woman like Gloria? Toni hoped not. But hadn't Jay found her attractive enough over the years? Even to the point of bringing her on a cruise where he hoped to effect a reconciliation with his wife for business purposes.

It had been stupid of him to do that, knowing how Toni felt about the blonde woman. And Jay was seldom stupid in his actions.

Depression pressed heavily on her again at the

very thought of Jay, and she was almost relieved when Marian said agitatedly at her side:

'Toni, this has all been a horrible mistake. I'm going down to my cabin and change into uniform.'

Toni stared at her in bewilderment. 'Change? But you look terrific! Why would you want to change?'

Marian's breath came in hurried snatches. 'Rick says I'm—letting him down. That as a m-member of the Purser's staff I should—display more dignity.'

'Dignity my foot!' snorted Toni, hardly aware of the silent figure that came to stand behind her left shoulder. Rick was being his pompous best if he had suggested that Marian looked less than gorgeous tonight.

The flapper outfit suited her beyond expectation, and Toni's own contribution of skilfully applied make-up had transformed her into a daring Twenties girl, complete with unlit cigarette in long black holder. 'Forget Rick,' she hissed forcefully, 'I've seen half a dozen men staring at you as if they'd like to know you better. Go out there and circulate.'

'But Rick——'

'Never *mind* Rick!' Toni said in an explosive undertone, mindful of the people thronging around them. 'A little jealousy never hurt anyone.'

'But——' Marian opened her mouth to protest again, only to stifle the sound in a muffled scream deep in her throat when the figure behind Toni stepped forward and said in a sibilant whisper:

'Would you care to dance with me?'

Toni herself reeled slightly at the sight of a well-set man, elegant in dark evening clothes, who stepped between her and Marian. He had all the attributes of a desirable male partner, except that —he had no head! The crisp white of his evening shirt ended abruptly in nothingness, with no matching head above the meticulously tied cravat around his neck.

Despite the prevailing sense of unreality, Toni shivered her apprehension. The man was an apparition from another life, another dimension. Marian, however, was surprisingly acquiescent as she giggled nervously and accepted the disembodied invitation to dance.

Mocking herself as the headless stranger cleared a path for himself and Marian on to the dance floor, Toni mentally numbered the costume entries. At no time had she noticed a headless man among the throng, though it was possible he had arrived too late for official entry into the competition. If he had been on time, she reflected with the expertise of long experience, he would have undoubtedly won first prize.

'Dance with me?'

Toni came out of her reverie to glance at the French seaman beside her. His impudent smile under rakishly set cap identified him as one of the young men she had escorted to their cabin on sailing day. She had seen little of them since then, and guessed that disco-ing in the Crowsnest Club until the small hours of the morning suited their taste more than the organised entertainment provided by the cruise staff.

'I'd be honoured,' she answered his infectious grin, and submitted to being threaded through the bystanders and on to the crowded dance floor.

'The honour is mine,' he bowed with exaggerated awe, putting a firm arm around her and drawing her closer. 'No wonder men lost their heads—literally!—over her, if she looked anything like you.'

'*Merci*, Monsieur Matelot,' she returned graciously, then added more realistically: 'She had a lot more power over men than I've ever had.'

He tilted his head to one side and appraised her critically. 'You're not ruthless enough,' he pronounced his verdict. 'A woman who wants that kind of power has to be hard, sure of herself.'

'You seem to know a lot about the subject,' Toni retorted, amused.

He shrugged. 'I've been around.'

As they moved closer to the centre of the floor, she noticed heads turning, shocked expressions turning to admiring smiles. The headless man, taller than any other male in the room, held a helplessly giggling Marian in his arms. Gloria, dancing sedately with Cyrus in his monk outfit, seared the couple with disdainful eyes, while a matronly woman to Toni's right openly admired the unknown man's costume.

'I didn't see him in the parade,' she said loudly. 'I wonder why? He'd have walked off with every prize there was.'

Her uncostumed husband grunted that it probably took the fool man two hours to get into the thing before they moved out of earshot.

'Why don't you come and sit at our table?' the pseudo-French sailor asked when the dance ended moments later.

'I'd love to,' Toni responded automatically, as she did to most invitations proffered by passengers, 'but I'm here to work, not enjoy myself.'

'Dedicated to duty, is that it?'

'Something like that.' Toni dashed off her cruise hostess smile and drifted away from the dance floor while chattering couples waited in suspended animation for the next dance to begin. A hand came out to lodge on her arm as she stepped towards the floor-side tables, and she swung round to look up into Rick's impassive face.

'May I impose on you for a dance?' He seemed more stilted than usual.

'That's no imposition, Rick.' She turned back and went into his stiffly held arms as the music began again. 'I like being with you,' she added simply, and winced as his hand tightened round hers.

'But only when Mr Gold-Plated Brownlea isn't around,' he jeered savagely. 'What happened, Toni? Did you scare him off with talk of marriage?' He gave a short laugh. 'Do you think a man like that marries every girl he sleeps with?'

Toni made an instinctive gesture of withdrawal, but Rick's grip tightened, pulling her closer to the stiff lines of his body. He put his lips to her ear, and to anyone watching, she thought almost hysterically, it must seem as if they were locked in a love embrace. But only the headless man was turned towards them and he, she thought with a nervously swallowed giggle, had no eyes to see with, no ears to hear with.

'Or was it only with me you were holding out for the marriage bit?' Rick grated at her ear. 'If only

I'd known you were so easy to get!'

This time Toni found the strength to wrench herself partially from him, her eyes blazing darkly up into his.

'I doubt if you'd have done anything about it, even then,' she threw blindly back with a cruel precision she regretted instantly. Rick's face darkened in a literal sense, and his hold on her slackened noticeably.

'You bitch!' he muttered hoarsely, and fastened his fingers round her neck, just above the golden medallion rested on her tanned flesh. 'I could kill you for that!'

His thumb slid upward and found her windpipe, gradually choking off her breath until she panicked and brought her own hand up in a useless effort to dislodge his. One part of her mind stood aside from the urgency of the situation and reflected on the ludicrous aspect. Was it possible that she could die here, in the midst of a crowd of dancers who were unaware of what was happening?

It was too ridiculous to contemplate, yet she and Rick seemed frozen in a macabre tableau that could only end in one way if the pressure he applied to her windpipe continued.

But it was not to be that way. At one moment she was held in a deathly grip, the next she was free, gasping and hearing Rick's hoarse:

'What the hell——?'

Time dissolved into a misty kaleidoscope of curious faces as she felt herself hurried through the lounge and the heavy doors leading to the deck, the fresh cool air coming as a balm to her fevered skin.

The deck rail was solid under her clutching fingers as she gulped the air generated by the ship's thrust through waters lit by moonlight.

As reality pierced the receding mists clouding her brain, Toni became aware of the silent man's figure behind her, of his arms loosely surrounding her, his gloved hands occupying the rail some distance from hers. Slowly she twisted round and looked up into what she had expected to be his face, and found nothing.

'Oh,' she said in choked resignation, 'it's you.'

The headless man, extraordinarily tall, asked in his sibilant whisper: 'Are you all right now?'

'Yes,' she nodded, turning her back to lean on the rail once more, her heart aching almost as much as the soft hollow at her throat. 'Thank you for—for what you did.'

The pause before he spoke lasted so long that she wondered if he had lost even the small vocal power he had possessed previously. She tried once again to place his identity among the passengers, and came up with a blank. He was noticeably taller than any of the people on board, even taller than Jay, who was a well-set six-two.

'What was the problem?' the penetrating whisper came at last.

Toni shuddered at the memory of Rick, the man she had always regarded as gently non-aggressive, placing his hand on her throat with the intention of cutting off life-giving air to her lungs.

'It was nothing,' she dismissed shakily, more for her own benefit than the stranger's.

'A man doesn't three-quarters strangle a girl

without due cause,' the whisper came back with an overtone of dry impatience. 'What really happened between you?'

The headless man came to stand beside her at the rail, and she glanced at the white edge of his collar, shrugging.

'I insulted him in a way men don't like to be insulted. It was my fault really.'

'What did he do to make you—insult him?'

Toni sighed wearily. 'Nothing tonight. But—he wanted to marry me, and I told him I was in love with someone else,' she paraphrased the last few days in her relationship with Rick. For the first time she recognised the value of a father confessor who was faceless, nameless. There was no one, anywhere, she could confide in with complete trust, apart perhaps from Carole.

'That's hardly a reason for throttling you,' he said in his odd half whisper. After a pause, he went on again. 'This other man you're in love with—does he know it?'

'Too well,' Toni replied bitterly. 'But he's the kind of man who makes use of that kind of information for his own ends. He'—she glanced again at her unlikely listener—'he's a business man, and he puts most of his feelings into that.'

'Has he never married?'

'Yes, he——' Toni stopped abruptly after an impulsive start. The man beside her was obviously a passenger or crew member—from his height, he could be one of the ship's burly engineers—and she had been less than discreet already. Whatever her need for an unbiased ear, she wasn't likely to find it aboard a ship isolated at sea.

The disembodied voice filled in the gap left by her sudden silence. 'If he cared enough about someone to marry her, surely he can't be all that absorbed in his business?'

'You weren't around all those times when he called to say he couldn't make the party he'd asked me to arrange,' she retorted acidly, then pushed away from the rail. 'If you'll excuse me, I should be getting back inside. I'm okay now.'

The man put one of his white-gloved hands on her arm. 'Will you dance with me?' he whispered.

Toni dropped her eyes from where his face should be and looked curiously at his white shirt front. His head must be down there somewhere, but there was no visible sign of it. It was a cleverly designed costume, one the owner must have brought aboard with him in anticipation of the masquerade party.

'All right,' she decided suddenly, smiling as she linked arms with him and felt the smooth hard muscles of his forearm. With muscles like that, he must be one of the brawny engine room crew members ... one who obviously thought she might guess his identity or he wouldn't have kept up his voice-straining whisper.

On the other hand, she reflected as they went back into the noisy ballroom, it might possibly be her reluctant exerciser, the Texan, Mr Branch. He was well set up and unusually fit, though the stranger at her side seemed quite a lot taller.

'I'm the envy of all the would-be Antonys in the arena,' he bent down to whisper in her ear. 'You're more beautiful than the original Cleopatra could ever have been. But tell me, where did all the piles of hair come from?'

'Haven't you ever heard of wigs and hairpieces?' she mocked, conscious of her brow-hugging curls and long black tendrils suspended from a knot at the back of her head. Her hair had been naturally long when she was married to Jay, and he had liked it that way. Long and silky when he ran his fingers through it. . . .

There was no sign of Rick's stiffly held figure among the dancers and she breathed a sigh of relief, still dazed from his attack. Though she couldn't really blame him, she told herself reproachfully as she circled the floor in the security of her strange partner's arms. Not too many men were willing to accept a slur on their manhood, which was virtually what she had done to Rick, blaming him for the restraint he had shown in their relationship.

'Your protegée seems to have burst out of her cocoon of mousiness,' her partner broke into her thoughts. 'She's having a high old time over there in the corner.'

Toni's eyes searched for and found an animated Marian ensconced between her own earlier partner, the French sailor, and his cabin-mate, making giggling efforts to smoke the king-sized cigarette they had lit in the holder. From a quick appraisal, Toni guessed that Marian had drunk more alcohol during this one evening that she had for the entire first part of her life.

'Oh, dear,' she murmured, 'I should go and rescue her. Those two could devour her for breakfast and still take their ham and eggs.'

'Wait,' her sibilant partner urged, tightening his hold on her gold-clad waist. 'I think somebody else is beating you to it.'

Toni's eyes swivelled again to that corner of the room and she saw a furious, tight-lipped Rick descend on the threesome. He grasped Marian by the elbow without ceremony and dragged her to her feet. An intense conversation followed, mostly one-sided from Rick, and at last Marian, looking subdued yet with an inner glow that clearly showed on the surface, looked apologetically back to the glowering younger men as she followed meekly behind Rick to the dance floor.

'Your strategy seems to have worked in that direction,' the headless man bent again to say.

Toni jerked away and stared at his white shirt front, the most visible part of him. 'How do you know what my strategy is?' she demanded suspiciously. 'There's something about you that——'

'Pardon me,' a matronly woman gushed from behind her, 'but aren't you Chuck Branch? My friends and I have made a little bet between us, and my guess is that you're the Texan who shares our table in the dining room.'

'Aw, shucks, ma'am,' came the unmistakable if somewhat muffled Texan drawl, 'I guess you're the winner of that little bet.'

'I knew it!' she crowed delightedly, and hurried off without another word to spread the news to her friends.

'So you *are* Mr Branch,' Toni commented, pleased that her own deduction had been correct.

'Chuck to you, honey,' he said with a breathtaking sweep of dance steps as the music ended. 'Will you have a drink with me?'

Toni hesitated for only a moment. One drink in his company wouldn't hurt. 'All right,' she nodded, smiling, 'but I can't stay too long, I'm——'

'I know. You're on duty, right? It's a positive sin the way they keep you gals working from morning till night,' he complained as he guided her towards a table for two at the rear. 'You take the exercise class early in the morning, and here you are still working.'

'I have time off in between,' Toni assured him, accepting the seat he held out for her. 'Besides, I love my job.'

'That's good.' He signalled a waiter hurrying by with an empty tray, then turned to ask Toni what she would like to drink, his whole body seemingly involved in the movement. The waiter registered her request for a Vokda Gimlet and the headless man's for Bourbon, a smile relaxing the harried lines of his face as he listened to the voice issuing from the shirt front.

'You should have entered the contest,' he said in a tone of amused admiration, 'you'd have won by a head.' Chuckling at his own wit, he rushed off in the direction of the bar.

'Wise guy,' the Texan grunted.

'I thought it was pretty clever on the spur of the moment,' Toni protested, her eyes returning to the shirt front. 'How in the world can you see through that shirt?'

'Dimly,' he retorted drily. 'I was told I'd be able to see right through it, but it's like looking up from under water.'

'Never mind,' she soothed, 'you can get rid of it at midnight—that's when all the masks come off and everyone is revealed as the person everybody knew they were anyway.' She glanced at the gold watch circling her wrist. 'That's in half an hour.'

'I may have to wait that long to swallow my drink,' he said wryly as the waiter returned and placed glasses before them.

'Maybe I could bring you a funnel, sir?' he enquired facetiously.

'That won't be necessary.' The Texan paid in cash, rather than signing for the bill, then raised his glass to Toni. 'Here's hoping.'

She was never quite sure afterwards how he did it, but at one moment the glass was full, the next it was empty. True, it had descended to the level of his chest, and one white-gloved hand had fluttered there for a moment, but for such a big man he was extremely dexterous.

'Do you always drink that fast?' she laughed.

'Only on occasions like this.'

'Have you been on many cruises?'

'This is the first.'

'You came alone?' she questioned delicately. 'I mean—you didn't bring your wife with you. If you're married, that is.'

'Well, I am and I'm not. Let's just say I'm pretty well in the same position as you.'

She look at him with sudden suspicion. Had she told him that she was married? She thought not. He seemed, however, to have read her mind.

'By that I mean that she wanted me to be something I couldn't be.'

Toni sipped at the tart-tasting vodka. 'She must have known before you married what kind of things were important to you.'

'Didn't you?'

Toni's dark-fringed lids dropped and her fingers tightened on the glass stem. The pointed question had sent a shock wave through her, leaving her no time to draw the usual defences round her like a cloak.

What she had just said to Chuck Branch applied equally to herself. She had married Jay knowing the kind of man he was, the things that were important to him. And then....

There was no movement under the smooth black jacket, but she sensed a shrug in the Texan's voice. 'It's hard for a woman not to want to change the man she marries, I guess.'

Toni raised her head and shook it, bewildered. 'But doesn't he have to change too when he marries? One of the main reasons for getting married in the first place is to be with each——'

'Well, howdy, honey,' a thick Texan drawl came from over her head. 'This sure beats the hell out of bendin' and stretchin' on the Sun Deck, don't it?'

CHAPTER EIGHT

Toni's slender shoulders stiffened and froze under the weighty arm. She needed no glance upward to know that the real Chuck Branch stood at her side of the table, no deep thoughts as to who sat opposite her. Who would have gone to the trouble of disguising his identity so well?

Jay! Anger rose in acrid sourness to her throat as she struggled to her feet.

'Meet your twin, Mr Branch,' she said thickly, 'or should I say, meet Mr Jay Stanford, alias James Brownlea!'

'Huh?' the rangy Texan asked drunkenly, but Toni stumbled away from the table, going in an erratic arc towards the heavy outer doors leading to the deck, ignoring Jay's 'Wait, Toni!' from behind.

He caught up with her as she skimmed along the deck close to the rail.

'For God's sake, Toni,' he grated, cursing the recalcitrance of the built-up shoulders he was trying to discard, 'stop and listen to me!' He pulled her up short with his hand on her upper arm.

'Listen to you?' she echoed hysterically. 'I'd be glad to if you'd just make up your mind who I'd be listening to! Jay Stanford? James Brownlea? Chuck Branch? The only one I can be sure you're not is the last one!'

The rail was slightly damp from the night air as

she gripped its smooth surface. Behind her she heard a muffled cursing as Jay divested himself of the disguise that had been so successful until the real Chuck Branch had suddenly put in an appearance. Where had the Texan, who hadn't dressed up, spent the earlier part of the evening? In one of the bars, she thought caustically, judging from his condition.

'Thank God for that,' said Jay fervently, stepping to the rail and smoothing his ruffled hair with impatient hands. 'I hope I never have to disguise myself again.'

'Why did you feel it necessary this time?' she queried acidly, turning her head back to where the sea foamed and hissed far below, lit by the ship's blazing lights. 'Or has double-dealing become a way of life with you now?'

His fingers closed tightly on her bare arm. 'If there's been any double-dealing, it's because you've forced me into it. From the state of your temper when I left the ship in Acapulco, it was hardly likely I'd find a warm welcome on my return. At least this way I'd have a chance to talk to you before you did your disappearing act again.'

'Why did you come back?' she asked dully, her voice as stiff as her tautly held shoulders. 'Did your Jacob Ansell insist on meeting your dearly beloved wife before signing the contract?'

Her eyes swivelled round and up, and she was scarcely surprised by the glint of puzzlement in his; it was more than obvious that he wouldn't have expected Gloria to tell her the real reason for his coming aboard.

'He wants to meet you, yes,' he said slowly, as if calculating the extent of her knowledge. 'He and his wife entertained me at their Palos Verdes estate, and——'

'And wondered why your wife didn't travel with you?' she finished for him scornfully. 'What did you tell him, Jay?—that I couldn't bear to leave my luxury cruise, even for my contract-hungry husband's sake?'

The hard line of his jaw grew steely, and it was a moment or two before he said in a carefully controlled voice: 'I can see you're in one of your unreasonable moods, and there's only one way to cope with them.'

There was a brief flare of pain as his fingers dug into her flesh, turning her to face him, his features unrelentingly hard as he dipped his head quickly to hers. Her mouth had opened in a gasp at the unexpectedness of it, and shock trembled through her when his lips made an easy conquest of hers.

Her vulnerable senses made an instant response, one she could no more resist than tides could ignore the moon's attraction. The hands she had raised to steady herself found the familiar warmth of his hard-muscled chest and became trapped between them when his hands slid over the glittering gold of her dress to her hips and drew her to the taut line of his thighs.

Desire leaped like a flame passed from his body to hers, crackling along her veins and rising to swell numbly in her throat.

A soft moan escaped her when Jay's hands released their pressure on her hips and came up in unison to clasp the fine bones of her ribcage.

One hand continued its upward motion, his fingers brushing warmly across her night-cooled skin to find the soft swell of her breast.

'No, Jay!' She pressed her hands against his chest with the steel strength born of panic and broke his loosened hold on her.

The fire that had been ignited in seconds between them now smouldered in his puzzled eyes as they seared hers, then went down to the soft tremble of her passion-swollen mouth.

'What?' he asked thickly, shaking his head slightly as if not believing what his ears had heard.

'This—doesn't solve anything,' she choked, willing her trembling legs to step back out of the orbit of his closeness, but they refused the command of her brain.

'I think it's a good start.' Jay's voice had steadied, and his head turned as an explosion of noise came from the far side of the deck. He frowned irritably.

'It's the conga,' Toni explained abstractedly. 'They—do a circuit of the deck before going back into the lounge.'

'That means they'll be here in a minute.' Jay caught her arm as she half turned. 'Come up to my stateroom,' he urged. 'We can talk there in peace.'

'Talk?'

'That's all, unless you want it any other way. It's time we talked, Toni. There's a lot of things that need to be——'

His voice was drowned out by the noisy procession that came round the forward part of the deck. The conga was led by the French sailor, and in another moment the snaking line of unmasked masqueraders was on them. Their leader bent sideways to pluck Toni from Jay's side.

'Come on, Cleopatra, we need some royalty to lead the parade!'

Toni's waist was held firmly between two strong male hands, and she had no choice but to fall into step at the head of the conga line.

Glancing back, her eyes met Jay's, but she had no time to diagnose the state of his feelings as she was thrust forward to the chanting line of merrymakers.

By the time they had traversed the outer deck, made a riotous re-entry into the ballroom, and out again to where she had been whisked from him, Jay had gone.

'He came back, didn't he?' Carole said lazily from her bunk. 'Doesn't that mean he cares about you? So what if he's never had any intention of buying the old *Queen*? Is the ship really what's important to you? If it is,' she rolled idly over on one arm, 'then you don't deserve the attention of a one-eyed toad, let alone a highly desirable male like Jay Stanford!'

Toni stared at her cabin-mate in amazement. It was the morning after the masquerade party, and the first surprise upon awakening after a restless night had been to see Carole asleep in her virginal berth. The morning exercise session now behind her, Toni stood between the beds in scarlet and white sweat suit.

'What made you change your tune so suddenly?' she asked suspiciously, lifting the heavy top over her head and throwing it on her own bunk. 'It seems like only yesterday you were telling me not to trust him—or any man, for that matter. Did Mike finally get through to you?'

'He wants to marry me,' Carole said starkly. 'Seriously.'

'And——?'

'I think I might. Is that crazy, after all I've said about men?'

Toni was careful in her reply. 'Not necessarily. Mike's a nice example of his species; I like him. He'd probably be good for you.'

'That's the strangest thing about it,' Carole said thoughtfully. 'I don't care whether he'd be good for me or not. All I want to do is to make him happy. Now do you think I'm crazy?'

'Yes.' Toni stepped out of the scarlet slacks. 'Crazy like all people in love are.' She forced a smile. 'When's the happy day to be?'

'You're as bad as Mike,' the other girl grumbled happily, 'trying to stampede me into a date.'

'You could always get Captain Vance to tie the knot for you, I suppose,' Toni teased as she went towards the bathroom, turning back just in time to catch Carole's grimace.

'The legality of that went out with "B" movies years ago! Though I wouldn't mind a service at sea. It would seem fitting somehow, you know?'

'The chaplain could do it, couldn't he?'

'I guess so, but——' Carole looked almost scared. 'Well, I know it sounds stupid, but I'm just terrified of making another mistake.'

Sensing her need to talk, Toni took her robe from

the wardrobe and shrugged into it as she came to
sit on her own bunk.

'You're in love with the guy, aren't you? I know
you pretty well after being cooped up with you for
two years in this apology for a cabin, and you've
never felt this way about anyone else. After all your
time at sea, you're not likely to have stars in your
eyes over the magic of moonlight on water.'

'That's just it,' Carole returned sombrely. 'I'm
so used to the atmosphere aboard that I don't know
if I could cope with shore life again.'

'The only way to find out is to try it,' Toni said
briskly. 'Sooner or later you're going to have to give
up the romantic way of life and set your feet firmly
on shore.' She hesitated. 'It's—unlikely Jay will take
on the *Queen*, and I don't think anyone else would
sink a fortune into her to keep her running. You
might be able to work for another line, but——'

'I'm getting to be over the hill, is that what you're
saying?' said Carole with a wry smile.

'Of course not. It might be difficult to find
another job as good as this one, that's all. As you
know, the competition is pretty fierce.'

'Mm. And what about you? What will you do
when the *Queen* berths in L.A. for the last time?'

Toni shrugged. 'I can always find work in the personnel department of a company like——'

'Like Jay's?' Carole finished softly. She made a
sudden, irritated movement to throw the covers off
and swung her feet to the floor. 'Why don't you wise
up, Toni, and admit you're in love with this man?
You were hooked right from the start, and you're
determined to dangle breathlessly on that hook for

the rest of your life! You're so tied up in non-essential details that you can't see the forest for the trees. So what if he seems more interested in his business affairs than you at times? If you're truthful, you'll admit that you fell in love with the very qualities you downgrade now—his ambition, his drive, his dedication to a dream of his, whatever it was.'

'You don't understand,' Toni said shakily, getting to her feet, deep-down honesty telling her that Carole understood only too well. She had told herself these home truths, but coming from Carole they had the power to sear, to hurt. 'All I wanted was a normal life, a husband home at night with me and our ch-children. He even wanted to fit children into his schedule so that his business concerns wouldn't be disturbed too much!'

Carole said nothing for a minute, then she put in gently: 'Maybe he didn't want children ... some men don't, you know.'

'But he did! He just wanted them at his own convenience, that's all.'

'Well, then maybe it was because he felt he could give them more of his attention when his business affairs were set up,' Carole reasoned.

'That's what he said,' Toni admitted slowly, 'but I—oh, Carole, you've no idea what it was like, sitting around all day just waiting for him to come home, and when we did have an evening together, Gloria would always find some excuse to call him. There were so many things,' she ended with a shrug.

Carole took her wrap from the end of her bed and slid her arms into it, saying drily:

'You have all my sympathy, honey, having to sit in your luxury penthouse like a princess locked in a castle! Really, Toni, your kind of woman makes me see red! There were plenty of things you could have done apart from nagging your husband into another woman's arms. You could have travelled with him, made a home out of the hotel rooms he had to come back to——'

'He didn't want me around,' Toni muttered angrily, knowing that the grievances that had been so important to her at the time were petty nonsense in Carole's eyes. 'He preferred Gloria's company to mine.'

'And you hadn't the intestinal fortitude to stand up for your rights then, any more than you have the guts to go up to his suite now and tell him you don't want to live in a world that doesn't include him!' Carole retorted inelegantly.

The two young women glared balefully at each other for a full minute, then the humour of the situation hit them simultaneously and they dissolved into helpless laughter.

'You think I can't do it?' Toni gasped at last.

'I think you *won't* do it.'

'Watch me!'

Pushing away the qualms that crowded in on her as soon as she was alone in the bathroom, Toni showered quickly and in another ten minutes was ready to leave the cabin. Fortunately her choice of clothes was simple, being the uniform skirt and top for duty after breakfast. She had taken care, however, to brush her hair into its customary shining cap and apply daytime touches of make-up which emphasised the deep sparkle in her dark eyes.

'Okay?' she enquired of a silent Carole when she reached the door and turned the handle with more confidence than she was feeling.

'Okay. I'll check in the Mariner Lounge after breakfast, and if you're not there to conduct the quiz, I'll know what's detained you.'

With the remains of a parting grimace still on her face, Toni went quickly along the passage to the elevator. She had to move swiftly, because her legs threatened to send her scurrying back to the safety of the cabin. It seemed fate that the elevator doors should be standing open waiting to receive her, but she pressed the button for two decks below Jay's. Walking up the remaining stairs would give her time to compose her thoughts and prepare her opening words.

But she was no nearer to finding the right words when she stepped from the elevator on the Boat Deck. 'Hello, Jay, I've just come to tell you that I love you and that——' And that what? That she would accept gladly the amount of time he had to spare for her?

Pride reared its overwhelming head. Could she bear to go back to being a small, however important, part of his life? Big enough to smother the jealousy that consumed her in knowing that Gloria fulfilled an essential niche in his business world, that their relationship would always exclude herself?

Her heart was racing when she pushed open the heavy doors giving on to the Special Suites, not entirely from the climbing of two flights of stairs. Resting for a moment with her back to the blank wall of the serving area, she paused to catch her breath.

Carole was right. Nothing else mattered but that she should be with Jay, the man she loved, whatever had come between them in the past. There would be a child—he had promised her that—and it was even possible that a microscopic new heart was beating within her right now. Their lovemaking aboard ship had been free and uninhibited, uncaring of consequences.

How often had she heard and read that a child was no way to prop up a sagging marriage? But perhaps in this case it was just the kind of catalyst Jay needed to channel his interest—or a large part of it —homeward, giving his child a warmer and more secure family background than he himself had ever known.

A door opened within the nest of suites, a woman's light voice sounding irritated in the exclusive hush of this part of the ship.

Toni pushed herself away from the wall and peeped around the corner. What she saw further down the wide passage made her eyes widen in heart-pounding disbelief.

Gloria, clad in a flimsy pale green negligee, was closing the door to Suite Six. Jay's suite.

'I thought you wouldn't do it,' Carole said drily from the dressing table, her back to Toni when she rushed into the room. 'You really are a—why, Toni, what is it? What's wrong?' Her blue eyes were immediately clouded with anxiety when she half turned and saw Toni's paled features.

'He—he wasn't alone,' she faltered, her lower lip

trembling. 'She—Gloria—was with him.'

'Oh, my God,' Carole breathed. 'You mean you walked in on them?'

Toni shook her head and stumbled across to her bunk, collapsing on it like a deflated balloon. 'She —was just leaving. In her nightclothes.'

She stared wide-eyed at the floor, seeing and hearing nothing except the inner mocking voice that told her Jay had lied to her when he had said Gloria meant nothing to him since his marriage. Obviously his 'nothing' hadn't included physical fidelity, something that seemed not so important to some men. Where the touch of another man might repel her, Jay was of the male breed that regarded lightly the physical attraction of another woman. And Gloria had physical attraction in spades.

'Toni, I'm sorry about this,' Carole drew Toni's attention with a light hand on her shoulder. 'But it doesn't necessarily mean anything important, does it? She's available as far as he's concerned, and she does nothing to hide that fact.'

Galvanised into sudden life, Toni cried hotly: 'Lots of men have made themselves available to me over the past two years, but I didn't throw myself into their beds!'

'It's different with men,' Carole consoled with a wry smile. 'The act of love can mean everything or nothing to them. Often it's a physical release, no more. And my guess is that Jay——'

'Save it, Carole.' Toni rose and paced the small cabin in an access of nervous energy. 'Jay's finished as far as I'm concerned. I never want to see him again.'

'That might be hard to accomplish on a ship surrounded by miles of ocean,' Carole reminded her acridly. 'Unless you want to hide out here in our mouse-sized suite, you'll have to——'

'That's exactly what I'll do!' Toni exclaimed excitedly. 'I'll stay down here until we get to Los Angeles, then I'll——'

'It's four more days until we reach L.A.,' Carole pointed out reasonably, 'and you *are* employed to entertain the passengers.'

'I don't care.' Toni threw her hands up dramatically, promising extravagantly: 'I'll take most of the duty next trip.'

'If there is a next trip,' Carole returned enigmatically, though her glance in Toni's direction was sympathetic. She moved to the door. 'I'll see that you're fed and watered for today, anyway.'

Toni belatedly thought of the questions her absence would arouse. 'Captain Vance—everybody—will be wondering what's happened to me.'

'I'll tell them you've developed some weird tropical disease.'

'What if they ask Dr Mackenzie for details?'

'I'll have primed him with some evasive answers,' said Carole, who was on a friendly basis with the crusty ship's doctor, a rarity on the crew level.

The cabin seemed suddenly desolate when Carole had gone. Toni moved restlessly back and forth between porthole to dressing table and flatly closed door. Hunger pangs sent plaintive messages from her stomach, pushing aside the searing vision of Gloria leaving Jay's stateroom a short while before. A healthy appetite unfed during the breakfast hour

made itself felt in actual pain by the time Carole
once again made an appearance. The bountifully
laden tray she carried made Toni reach forward
eagerly to take it from her.

'If only your sympathisers could see you now,'
Carole commented drily. 'Everybody from the Captain on down has sent messages of condolence.'

Toni gnawed hungrily on a delicately seasoned
chicken thigh. 'Mmm,' she mumbled, 'this is wonderful.'

'Your husband seems particularly concerned
about you,' Carole threw out with deliberation, her
blue eyes reflecting her curiosity.

'You saw Jay?' Toni dropped the denuded bones
to her plate and looked at Carole with hesitant ex-
pectancy. Appetite appeased momentarily, she felt
the return of the twisting knot in her midriff. It was
only too easy for her to picture Gloria in Jay's arms,
in his bed, all night long. The thought of his hands,
his mouth, inciting Gloria to ecstasy had been
like a stone in her throat all morning.

'I can just imagine how concerned *he* was,' she
said caustically to the hovering Carole. 'Can't you
see that he's only concerned about the deal he has
cooking in L.A.? The man who controls the strings
is a strict—whatever his religion is. As far as Jay's
concerned, he needs a wife to bump him up to
multi-millionaire status. That's it. Period.' She
looked down sourly at the remainder of her lunch,
her appetite gone now.

'I think you're wrong,' Carole gave back posi-
tively. 'He didn't seem at all the way you describe
him. I like him,' she added with effective defiance.

'He was genuinely concerned about you.'

'He has a lot of power to charm when it suits him, too,' Toni retorted drily, recognising the familiar signs of Jay's effect upon women. As Carole turned back to the door, she added contritely: 'Carole—thanks. For the lunch.'

The other girl waved a dismissing hand. 'Don't mention it. I'm going to stoke up myself now in preparation for the afternoon's torture session at the pool.' She was referring to the final meet of the children's swimming competitions, an activity usually supervised by Toni.

'I'm sorry.' Toni started to get to her feet, but Carole waved her back.

'Stay where you are. You're making a much greater impression in certain quarters by hiding away down here.'

Making an impression in any quarter was far from what Toni had intended, but she let Carole go after a cautionary word about some of the participants in the afternoon swim-off. There was always a minor element of hard-to-handle children, and on this cruise Tommy Warren, the eleven-year-old son of a professional couple, was the ringleader of a small but troublesome group.

'I'll hang him head down over the rail if he gives me any problems,' Carole told her sourly as she left the cabin, and Toni subsided on her bunk, not knowing whether to be sorry for Carole, who had little patience in the handling of children, or for Tommy Warren. On balance, she would weigh Carole's no-nonsense outlook favourably against the youngster's effervescent spirits.

The cabin, far from the upper deck efficiency of
air-conditioning, was warm, close, claustrophobic,
and Toni thought longingly of the spacious air-
cooled lounges far above. Her complaints about the
staff quarters on the *Aztec Queen* had never held
much force, because she normally spent so little
time in the confined cabin.

Now, the cream-painted steel bulkheads seemed
to crowd in on her, the heat stifling her into inertia.
Not even the thought that Jay was somewhere above
her could prop the heavy drag of her eyelids open.
She lay back against the pillow and drifted pain-
lessly into sleep.

The stridency of an alarm bell broke into Toni's
dreamless sleep, and she started up on the bunk,
heart pounding and blinking the remnants of
drugged torpor from her eyes.

Her trained senses recognised instantly that the
emergency was not one concerned with the safe progress of the ship. The intermittent alarm denoted
a lesser emergency ... like the accidental falling of
a body overboard.

Almost before her depressed senses had registered
that fact, she was on her feet and running. Passengers were crowding the closed elevator doors,
their alarm manifest in the jumbled mixture of
bodies, life-jackets slung haphazardly over sleeveless blouses and gaily patterned short-sleeved shirts.

'Please—there's no cause for alarm,' Toni raised
her voice above the panicked uproar.

'So why is that bell ringing?' a grey-faced man
asked her truculently.

The hysterical chatter died down as the others turned for guidance to Toni's confident tone.

'If you'd paid attention to the lifeboat drill,' she chided, 'you'd have known that this warning bell is for something entirely different.'

'Like what?' the man beside her questioned sceptically. 'Pirates coming aboard?'

'It's possible someone has fallen overboard, but——'

Anxiety flamed again instantly, fired by concern for family members on the upper decks.

'It's probably one of the crew members,' Toni soothed, adding tongue in cheek: 'It's happened before, and the man was rescued with no trouble. Now please don't——' Her voice faded into obscurity as the elevator doors opened and the crowd surged inside, threatening to overload the mechanism. Abandoning the effort as futile, she made for the sweep of stairs leading from one deck to the other.

Crowds swarmed around one section of the Boat Deck despite the crewman's efforts to clear space. One of the lifeboats was missing, like an absent tooth in an otherwise perfectly symmetrical set. The rail gates were open to the sea, and the press of onlookers threatened to send the crewman over the side.

Toni forced her way to the rail, grumbling passengers giving way at sight of her uniform. Newcomers jostled the backs of the first arrivals, their questions answered in the superior way of those in the know.

'One of the kids fell overboard.'

'A passenger jumped right in after him, but it took a while for the ship to slow down.'

'The lifeboat's almost there.'

Some distance from the ship, and to its rear, Toni saw the lifeboat approaching two barely discernible heads bobbing around on the forceful swell of the ocean. Relief flowed over her. The two overboards would be saved.

Lightened of pressure, she took her eyes from the dramatic scene being enacted offside to glance at the spectators lining the rail. Many of the passengers were familiar to her, and there was Carole at the other side of the opened section, comforting Tommy Warren's mother, a slender dark-haired woman in her late thirties.

So Tommy was the child overboard! Toni wasn't surprised. She even felt a smile twitch at her lips. Had Carole fulfilled her threat to hang him over the side by his heels if he caused her any trouble?

Gloria stood against the rail with fixed gaze on the rescue scene. Cyrus was behind her, but of Jay there was no sign. Immersed as he was in his own world of big business, she thought acidly, a minor accident at sea would hold no interest for him.

At the moment that thought crossed her mind her eyes swept back to where the lifeboat had reached the hapless pair, and she saw two sinewy arms reach up to hand the boy into the waiting crewman's grasp. A collective sigh went up from the audience lining the rail.

'He got him!' a man beside Toni exulted. 'That guy deserves a medal!'

'Who is it?'

'I don't know, but whoever he is he's going to be the cruise hero! Oh, my God, will you look at that?'

Toni did look, and was appalled by what she saw. One of the crewmen tended to the rescued boy while the others grabbed wildly for the rescuer, who seemed to have disappeared after handing the boy to the boat crew.

It seemed ages later when the man's limp body was hauled aboard the lifeboat.

'Something must have happened to him,' the passenger beside Toni turned to her as a source of information. 'Are there sharks in these waters?'

'It's most unlikely,' Toni responded in an automatic defence against the alarmed looks of passengers in their vicinity. 'He's probably just exhausted from the long swim to save the boy.'

The crowd fell silent as the lifeboat approached the ship and manoeuvred alongside. Toni knew, long before the winches went into action to levitate the small boat to deck level, that the man lying supine between the seats was Jay.

CHAPTER NINE

JAY was still unconscious when they took him below to the ship's hospital. The dark bruise already forming between his brows explained the blotting out of consciousness when an angry wave tossed him against the rock-hard side of the small boat as it fought for stability in the swelling seas.

The two-bed hospital ward was already inundated with people by the time Toni, delayed by Carole's request to help her clear the dack, reached it. Dr Mackenzie was straightening away from Jay's inert figure on the iron bedstead, bushy eyebrows plunging as they surveyed the gathering which consisted of the Captain, Gloria, Cyrus, Rick, and the four-member rescue team who had come below to follow their charge's progress.

'There's nothing any of you can do for him now,' he told them briskly. 'He's had a hard knock on the head, but he'll come round in time. I want everybody out of here.'

'But not me, surely, doctor?' Gloria enquired frostily. 'He'll want to see me when he comes round.'

'Are you his wife?'

'Well, no, but——'

'I'm his wife,' Toni said from the doorway.

She hardly noticed the shocked silence that greeted her announcement. Her senses were all alerted towards the silent figure on the bed, skin pale under the beginning tan on lean cheeks. It was Captain Vance who broke the stillness.

'Toni, you're not well, you don't know what you're saying,' he came towards her with out-stretched hand. 'Maybe you should have the doctor look you over while you're here.'

'I don't need the doctor,' she insisted stubbornly, her eyes never leaving Jay's still figure. 'Jay's my husband, and it's my right to be with him.'

Gloria, her face a rigid mask, broke in furiously: 'It's a pity you didn't stand on your rights two years ago when you left him!'

Toni slowly turned her eyes on Gloria, ignoring the stunned expressions of the others in the room. Her mouth twisted bitterly.

'It was because of your lies that I left him. I should have listened to him, not your insinuations that had no basis in truth.'

'Truth?—what do you know about the truth?' Gloria's voice had risen to a high pitch. 'Jay and I have been lovers ever since I started with his company! Why do you think he took me and not you on all his business trips?'

'I will not have this brawling in my hospital.' Dr Mackenzie intervened testily. 'I want everybody out, except my patient's wife.'

'Remind me at a later date to raise your salary,' a weak, only half audible voice came from the bed.

Gloria started forward. 'Jay darling, are you all right?' she crooned, placing a well manicured hand on one of the dark-haired forearms outside the blankets.

Still without opening his eyes. Jay said wearily: 'I will be as soon as I'm left alone with my wife, as the good doctor said.'

'But, Jay——'

It was Cyrus who came forward from the side of the room to take Gloria's arm and lead her away. His right eye gave a definite wink as they passed Toni, and she knew he would keep the woman well away from the hospital room.

Captain Vance put a fatherly hand on Toni's shoulder. 'I don't pretend to know what's going on here,' he said gruffly, 'but I hope whatever it is is the right thing for you.'

Toni nodded and forced a smile, her eyes going to where Rick hesitated by the door. There was a look half baffled, half accusing about him, but he managed an acknowledging nod before passing out of the room.

The crewmen had already left, and only the doctor remained. Clearing his throat, he cast one backward look at his patient and stomped to the door.

'You can talk in freedom,' he stated, a twinkle lighting the hidden depths under his craggy brows. 'I'll see you're not disturbed.'

The silence after he left was total, and Toni seemed frozen to the spot. For all her confidence with Gloria moments before, her limbs were now paralysed with uncertainty.

'Are you going to stay there all day, or are you going to take advantage of the doctor's offer of privacy?'

Her head lifted to where Jay, his eyes opened wide, mocked her from the bed.

'I—maybe you should rest for a while,' she faltered.

'Rest be damned!' he exploded in his normal voice, all traces of weakness gone. He lifted an imperative hand. 'Come over here.'

Her legs moved of their own volition, and when she would have stood meekly beside the bed his arm shot out and pulled her down beside him. His thigh under the covers was hard and warm against hers.

She resisted the sudden urge to touch the firm contour of his jaw where a beginning darkness of beard was beginning to show. Too many hurts and misunderstandings lay between them for her to take the initiative now. Questions lay like a coiled snake inside her, the residue of past and present pain collecting like a pulsing ball in her midriff.

'Why did you pretend to be ill today?' Jay asked softly, his fingers ploughing through the dark cap of her hair, drawing her head round so that she was forced to look directly into his eyes.

'I wasn't really pretending,' she prevaricated, smudgy black lashes falling so that her gaze was centred on the firm outline of his mouth.

And that was worse, if anything. She ached to feel the warm pressure of his lips on hers, the shivering anticipation as they descended to throat and breast, their intimate caress inviting her to partake in the heady banquet he offered.

'You seem fine now,' he pointed out, huskily reasonable.

Toni herself felt the glow that lit her eyes and sent soft colour to her cheeks. A glow that stilled all questions, that made nonsense of doubts.

'Not here,' she breathed, alarmed when Jay's fingers accurately found the zipper pull of her top and slid it down to its furthest extent, his hands, warm and strong on her shoulders, urging its downward motion.

'Why not?' he husked with lazy confidence, his fingertips tracing the white lace trim of her bra in a tantalising arc. 'The doctor promised us privacy.'

'I know, but——' Toni summoned her rapidly dispersing willpower and drew herself forcibly back against the hand he held at her back. 'Jay, we have to talk first. As I said last night, making love doesn't solve anything.'

'It could solve my problem of the ache you left with me last night,' he murmured wryly, and her colour deepened.

'Jay, it's more important that we—talk first. I——'

'Are you putting conditions, Toni?' his voice grew harsh. 'What happened to all your talk to Gloria a few minutes ago? Something about trusting my actions more than her words?'

'I *want* to trust you, Jay,' she said miserably. 'It's just that——'

'We'll talk later,' he insisted with hard-jawed stubbornness, pulling her easily down until she nestled comfortably in the circle of one arm, the other efficiently divesting her of the confinement of clothing until her high-peaked breasts met the firm flesh of his bared torso. 'You don't know what torture you've put me through,' he muttered fiercely against the soft underline of her throat, 'playing hard to get.'

'But I——' The rest of her words were lost in his sudden commandeering of her mouth with lips that parted the tender outlines of hers with harsh demand and forced the response she was helpless to deny.

Her firmly toned muscles dissolved into jelly when he turned her in the narrow confines of the hospital bed and began the slow, exquisitely familiar process of making love to her, adoring every peak, each shadowed indentation until conscious thought merged into feeling, feeling into a mindless need to give ... and receive.

Storm gave way to golden aftermath, like the low-lying sun slanting through the hospital's portholes. Toni, spent, lay in the circle of Jay's arms and knew the joy of fulfilment, his head cradled on the sun-browned skin of her shoulder. The utter contentment that came from the knowledge that this man was hers, completely and irrevocably, pushed aside her doubts as if they had never been.

Jay, however, seemed far from content to leave it there. Lifting his head, and kissing lazily from the vulnerable line of her throat to the veiled darkness in her eyes, he said huskily:

'How could you ever believe that any other woman could hold a candle to you where I'm concerned? Gloria least of all.'

Toni struggled back to remembrance of the concerns that had plagued her for so long they seemed like a part of her. Hazily, she offered: 'I saw her leave your stateroom this morning. She looked—

very attractive in that green negligee.'

Jay looked into her eyes from a distance of inches, his jaw hardening. 'And you thought—what, exactly?'

She blinked, then veiled her eyes with her lashes. 'What do you think? That she'd—spent the night with you. Didn't she?'

Her eyes opened wide then, and saw the deep flare of anger at the back of his eyes. With a muttered oath, he rolled over to stare bleakly at the cream-painted ceiling.

'You still don't trust me, do you?' he asked at last in a weary tone.

'I do, Jay, really I do,' she put in swiftly, then went on more hesitantly: 'It's just that——'

'That you half believe all that baloney she spouted off here a while ago. For God's sake, Toni,' he turned his head to let her see the bleak anguish in his eyes, 'don't you know by now that you're the only one who means anything to me in that way? Sure, we had a short-lived affair when she first came to the company ... she's an attractive woman, she packages herself well. But there's more to a woman than the outer wrappings, as I found out when I met you for the first time.'

'I thought,' Toni whispered, at the same digesting the heady import of his words, 'you'd turned to her because of—because of last night. I didn't want to leave you, Jay, but I *am* employed by the line to keep the passengers happy.' Her lashes fell again to make black arcs on her cheeks. 'I was on my way to your stateroom this morning to tell you that I— that I love you, no matter what.'

Jay lay rigidly at her side for an interminable time before he said tautly: 'And when you saw Gloria leave my room in her nightclothes, you naturally jumped to the conclusion that she'd spent the night with me. In the same way you assumed that she was my mistress on the business trips we took together.'

Toni's clear brown eyes hung on his. 'She's just said that——'

'Why do you find it so hard to believe me,' he interrupted brusquely, 'when you're willing to credit every damn thing Gloria tells you?'

He pushed back the covers and sprang from the narrow bed, covering himself with the white terry robe laid across a chair back. His hands automatically patted the pockets of the unfamiliar garment for the cigarettes he obviously felt in need of at that moment, then he ran a frustrated hand through his dark hair.

'Don't you think I'd have married her years ago if I'd wanted her in my life?' he exploded, wheeling back to the bed and ignoring Toni's bare shoulders that were dark against the white sheet she held to her.

'Not necessarily,' she returned evenly. 'Gloria's an attractive woman, but not the meek and mild type you like in a wife.'

Jay stared at her in dumb amazement for several moments before throwing his head back in a crowing laugh. Creases of amusement still bordered his mouth and eyes when he sat on the edge of the bed, one black brow raised sardonically.

'Are you saying that's the kind of wife you were?

Your memory must have suffered a lapse, because I distinctly recall having to fight every inch of the way, including marrying you to get you into bed with me.'

'That's what I mean,' Toni cried, turning restlessly on the pillow, avoiding his intent gaze. 'You'll go to any lengths to get what you want, even to—c-coming aboard this ship on the pretext of buying it just so that you could produce a wife and get the contract.'

Jay was silent for so long that she turned her head and sent a darting glance at his whitely set face. Why did he have to look so thunderstruck, when what she had accused him of must be true? Whatever faults Gloria possessed, none of them included ignorance of any part of Jay's business.

At last he spoke, in an icy voice that sent cold splinters into her heart.

'Get dressed,' he ordered abruptly.

'Wh-why?'

'Because I have no intention of parading my wife through the ship in her present state,' he grated.

He stood grimly by while she fumbled over her dressing, then, making no attempt to send for his own clothes, which would still be wet in any case, he put a hand under her elbow and marched her to the door.

Curious glances followed their progress in the hall and at each stop of the elevator on its way to the Special Deck above. Jay ignored them all, and hustled Toni silently along the wide passage leading to his suite. Once there, he propelled her firmly to one of the comfortable armchairs flanking the wide windows, settling her there firmly but not ungently.

Still without speaking, he retraced his steps into the bedroom and she heard drawers being opened and slammed shut, the wardrobe doors slammed back, and wondered if the knock on his head had temporarily deranged his mind.

However, when he came back dressed in fresh shirt and slacks he looked normal, apart from the livid bruise on his forehead. In his hand he held a lit cigarette, and he walked with his rapid strides across to the small bar. Without asking her preference he poured a vodka-based drink for her and a stiff whisky for himself.

'Should you be drinking?' she ventured as she reached up automatically to take the drink she hadn't asked for. 'That's quite a bruise you have on your head.'

'I'm all right,' he answered impatiently, and went to stand by the window across from her chair. For a short while he seemed mesmerised by the blue-green sea whipping past down below, then he sighed and said heavily: 'I didn't come back to the ship and go through all that rigmarole with the costume just to soften you up for the contract kill. The fact is, you weren't needed for any part of the deal. Jacob Ansell is a religious man, but he's also a business-man—a hard-headed one.'

'But you—you said he wanted to meet me,' stammered Toni, her drink untouched on the small side table.

Jay swung round to give her a bleak look. 'He did ... purely on a social level. He and his wife were hospitality itself when I was in L.A., and asked me to bring you to see them when we get back to the States. The deal was already fixed when I left. So you see,' he turned back to the window again, 'I didn't come back for that reason.' He lifted the glass of whisky and took a deep drink from it. 'But I don't suppose you'll believe that any more than you've seen fit to trust me in any important way during our marriage.'

'I—I believe you,' Toni whispered. How could she not, when he was standing there saying these things as if they didn't matter to him any more? As if she didn't matter to him any more!

He ignored her gulped words as if she hadn't spoken. 'And while we're on the subject of trust, you might as well know the whole story. I'd been looking forward to bringing back a piece of news I thought would make you happy, and maybe——' He broke off and tossed the remainder of the whisky down his throat.

'Jacob and I,' he said from the bar as he refilled his glass, his back to her, 'after a couple of late-night sessions, came to an agreement about taking over the *Aztec Queen* and making her into a paying proposition.' Again he ignored Toni's gasp. 'As a matter of fact, that's why you saw Gloria coming from my stateroom early this morning. She had directed all my messages to herself while I was away, so Jacob's wire of confirmation came to her.'

'Oh, Jay!' Toni was stunned, unable to think or to articulate the words even if her brain hadn't suddenly stopped functioning. Filling the void was a dull roar, like the sound of the sea coming from a distance.

'So that's it, Antonia!' Jay walked back towards her, the dead look in his eyes sending icy fingers of fear down her spine. She hardly knew him like this.

'Jay, please—don't be this way,' she pleaded. 'I'm sorry ... I misjudged you, I know, but——'

'But nothing!' He reached down and pulled her forcibly from the chair by her elbows, the hard tips of his fingers biting into her flesh. 'A man expects certain things from his wife, just as she expects certain things from him. Right at the top of my list is the quality of trust she places in him, and on a score of one to ten you'd come in at zero!' He shook her slightly, then let her go so that she fell back into the chair.

Toni's dormant state gave way to a swift spurt of anger. 'What about my expectations?' she flared, colour rushing up to deepen the tan on her cheeks. 'I had the right to expect at least a little of my husband's time! Everything else in your life was important to you except me! It needs no feat of the imagination to guess that you didn't even miss me for days after I left you! Or did you come back to our so-called home to change your socks?'

'I missed you,' he gritted, 'but I decided to let you grow up a little, even though you had run back to mama and papa and weren't likely to change into a woman from the spoiled brat you were.' He ran a weary hand through his hair when tears sprang to her eyes. 'I'm sorry about your parents, I know how much they meant to you. But the fact remains that they brought you up to be such a narrow-minded young woman that you weren't fit to be my or anybody else's wife!'

'I didn't notice too many complaints in the bedroom!' she threw back as she bounced to her feet and glared at him.

'There's more to marriage than sex, as you've told me so often.' Jay made a dismissing gesture with his hand and went back to contemplating the ocean. 'This isn't getting us anywhere, it's like the replay of an old record. I was wrong when I thought we could make a new start. Instead we'll just be one more statistic in the divorce records.'

'That suits me just fine!' Toni snapped, whirling round so fast that her hand caught her untouched drink and sent it tumbling to the floor. Ignoring it, she marched to the outer door and let herself out of the suite. Just outside the door she lost the impetus of her anger and leaned weak-kneed against it, her lids blinking against the avalanche of tears that threatened to cascade down her cheeks.

She managed to pull herself upright when there was a crash of glass against the wall from inside the suite. Her main regret as she walked unsteadily along the passage was that she hadn't relieved her explosive feelings in the same way.

Carole was more beautiful than Toni had ever seen her as she stood before the improvised altar in the main lounge. Mike's stalwart figure beside her. Her blue linen dress, simple in style but well-cut, emphasised the blue of her eyes. One of the passengers had donated a wisp of a hat that perched like froth on her blonde head, and Toni's heeled evening slippers adorned her feet.

As the chaplain began to speak. Toni's eyes wandered around the packed lounge where magnificent displays of flowers had appeared from all over the ship. The normal lounge chairs had been arranged in rows, and every seat was filled, the first two rows being reserved for crew members.

Marian, flushed to a becoming pink, was next to a serious-looking Rick. He was wearing his best uniform, but Marian had blossomed forth in a multi-coloured dress of sheer nylon. The transformation from mousy Assistant Purser to attractive woman was complete, and Toni felt a faint twinge of envy when Marian's eyes met Rick's in a smile which excluded the rest of the world.

'Do you, Carole, take this man . . .'

Toni's mind wandered as the solemn service proceeded. Carole had been too full of her suddenly decided wedding plans two days before to notice Toni's tautly drawn face, the deep misery in her eyes.

Much more exciting for the blonde girl was the chaplain's agreement to perform the ceremony on board ship, the Captain's gladly given permission to commandeer the main lounge for the event, and Rick's suggestion that closed circuit television could be set up in the areas adjoining the lounge for the overflow.

And overflow there was, Toni reflected, glancing back at the filled rows. A wedding aboard ship was an unexpected bonus on their cruise, one they would tell their friends about for years to come.

Her throat contracted when her eyes encountered and held to Jay's. He was in the privileged first row, on the Captain's right, and handsome as she remembered him in dark business suit and crisp white shirt.

Even with a superhuman effort, she found that

her eyes refused to break the almost tangible force that stretched between them. It was as if they were repeating their own marriage vows ... Jay had looked just that way at her then, as if she were the most precious being in his world.

Only now there was an added quality in his steady return of her gaze. His eyes were—regretful? —accusing? He had told her once that he could tell what she was thinking just from looking into her eyes. What could he see in them now? That she loved him now and always had? That she regretted the inexperienced, self-centred girl she had been on their wedding day and for most of the brief time they had been together?

Jay deliberately turned his head back to the front, and Toni felt anew the wrenching misery that had eaten into her for the past two days. That had been more than enough time to stand aside from her own hurt pride and see that she had never known the true meaning of love between married people until it was too late. She had wanted to fit Jay into a mould made to measure for her own father, who had found his happiness in an undemanding job that freed him to enjoy the family life he loved.

But Jay wasn't like her father in any way, had never known the warm security of loving parents and a stable home. It had been up to her to lay the foundations of a loving environment uniquely theirs, but instead ...

'... may kiss the bride.'

Mike kissed Carole in a way that brought a lump to Toni's throat, and her eyes automatically sought Jay's again, but his seat on the front row was empty. When had he left?

Her mind was only half on the well-wishing of the crew and passengers as they crowded round the newly-wed couple in the lounge, and later in the larger dining room which had been laid out buffet-style for the sumptuous reception.

The ship's chefs had excelled themselves at short notice, producing a massive six-tiered cake expertly decorated with swans and cherubs. There were glazed hams, chickens ringed with succulent peeled oranges on elevated trays, an abundance of cold meats arranged attractively on oval platters, vegetable and pickle dishes, all interspersed freely along the huge banquette. A tempting array of desserts ended the display, their colours vying with flower arrangements scattered here and there on the table.

'It makes me wish we could have ours all over again,' sighed a plump middle-aged woman.

'We couldn't have afforded it then, and we can't now,' her mate retorted, but his hand was gentle on her elbow as he urged her towards the feast.

'Well, hi, honey!' a breezy male voice said from Toni's side. 'Why are you standing here all on your lonesome? The food looks a mite picky, but I reckon it'll hold us off till dinner.'

Toni had little choice but to let herself be swept along by Chuck Branch, who piled her plate liberally with tempting morsels.

Toni, uninterested in the food, let her eyes wander to the many familiar faces clustered round the table. Gloria was there with a jovial Cyrus, Marian with Rick, and when the Texan's table companions descended on him with cooing cries, she escaped to a far corner of the dining room where she could search for Jay more freely.

As time wore on, the fount of champagne dispensed by the circulating stewards loosened tongues and sent the volume of noise up to screaming pitch. It was obvious Jay wasn't here. She could pick him out of any crowd in a minute.

Her mouth had frozen into the stiffness of a formal smile by the time Carole and Mike took their places behind a separate table for the cake-cutting ceremony. Flashbulbs popped as the happy couple posed with hands on knife, then there was a general surge forward as the guests lined up for individual slices cut by a bakery assistant.

Toni was swept along in the mass migration to the small side table where the massive cake's tiers were being rapidly diminished. She had picked up her own slice and was moving away when Carole came from the far side of the table.

'Give her another portion, Rico,' she instructed the assistant, smiling as she looked into Toni's puzzled eyes. 'Jay doesn't seem to be here, but I'd like him to have a piece of our wedding cake.'

'Oh. He—doesn't care much for fruit cake,' Toni responded weakly.

'He might, if you take it to him,' Carole suggested softly. 'I just hate the idea of him being all alone when I'm so happy.'

Tears stung the back of Toni's eyes. 'I hope you'll always be as happy as you are now,' she said unevenly, and a wry smile spread over Carole's features.

'I won't be. But at least I'll have all this to look back on when I feel like sticking a carving knife into Mike instead of the turkey!' She picked up the extra portion Rico had provided and handed it to Toni. 'Take it to him,' she urged. 'It can't do any harm, and it might do a lot of good.'

'Carole, I told you——'

'I know, I know, it's all over between you. But please don't refuse me on my wedding day.'

Toni sighed, then smiled. 'All right. Thanks.'

She was blinking back tears as she pushed her way through the surrounding crowd. Jay should have married somebody like Carole, who had no false expectations where marriage was concerned, who accepted that there would be times when the romantic overtones were submerged in the ups and downs of daily living.

CHAPTER TEN

THE Special Deck held an added hush when Toni walked along its wide passage bearing two portions of the wedding cake. Even more forbidding was the dark polished wood of Jay's door with the gold lettering denoting the suite number.

Balancing the two plates in one hand, she knocked tentatively with the knuckles of the other. Absolute silence greeted her and she turned away, half relieved that Jay was perhaps in one of the public rooms. She had no idea of what she would have said to him anyway. Her pride had not been so totally discarded that she would beg on her knees for another chance to make things work between them.

A door clicked shut somewhere inside the suite, and she lifted her hand to knock again, swallowing hard. This time she was rewarded by an irritable 'Come in!'

The door yielded to her trembling fingers, and as she closed it behind her she discerned Jay's broad-shouldered figure at the far side of the bed. He was picking up the suit jacket he had evidently discarded there earlier, but his hand froze in mid-air when he saw who his visitor was. His expression was obscured in the dimmer bedroom light, but his body obviously tensed.

'I—brought you some wedding cake,' she offered

lamely, lifting the hand holding the two plates.

The irony hidden in his face was more evident in his voice. 'What brought on this sudden wifely concern? Or do I have to ask?' He dropped the jacket back on the bed and walked into the sitting room, saying over his shoulder: 'Don't women always get nostalgic at other women's weddings?'

'I guess so.' Toni ventured further into the room, leaving the dark-grained fruit cake on the bedroom dresser before slowly following him into the living area. 'But that's not why I came.'

Jay picked up a cigarette package from the coffee table and lit one before turning to let his eyes flicker over the white of her low-necked dress. 'You look more like the bride than the bride did,' he observed drily. 'So why did you come?'

'Because I——' Toni paused and bit her lip. Whatever she said at this moment would sound trite and contrived. 'Jay, I want us to—to have a new start, to—begin all over again.'

Once started, she seemed unable to stem the words that rushed to her lips to be aired. 'I was too young, too inexperienced, too—selfish to know then that—that I shouldn't try to change you into someone you could never be.' She made a futile gesture with her hands. 'I wanted you to be like my father, that nothing was more important to you than your home and family.' Her voice dropped a notch or two. 'But I also wanted you to be the man I'd fallen in love with, the man who built an empire by his own efforts. I—expected too much of you.'

The humbling of her spirit was complete, but Jay still made no move towards her, no gesture of understanding. He hadn't even looked at her since she had started to speak. Now he did, his expression guarded.

'What makes you think things would be any different this time around?'

Toni's heart skipped a beat, and then another. At least he hadn't closed his mind—or maybe it was his heart—to the possibility of her proposal.

'I can't give any guarantees,' she whispered, her voice thickening as tears gathered in her throat. 'I can't even say I won't feel jealous of Gloria any more. I just know that I—I love you ... I need you ...'

His voice cut harshly through her faltering words. 'Come here!'

She lifted her head and looked at him as he stood silhouetted against the brightness outside. She had to peer to gauge that his expression denied the hard note in his voice.

'Come here,' he said again more gently. As if to entice her, he opened his arms, and she needed no second bidding. Giving a strangled cry, she stumbled across the floor and into the haven he offered.

'I'm sorry, Jay,' she sobbed against the hard wall of his chest, her arms clamped around his waist, her hands clutching the white cloth of his shirt, 'but I mean to—to make it up to you. I've been so foolish.'

'I have a lot to make up for too, sweetheart,' he said against her hair, cradling her in his arms. 'I expected too much of you too.' He lifted his head and forced her chin up with gentle fingers. 'Where do you think I was going when you came in just now?' he asked huskily.

Toni shook her head. 'I don't know. Where?'

'To come and find you and say the same kind of things you've just said to me.' His mouth twitched in a wry smile. 'You just beat me to it.'

'Oh, Jay!' Her entire body seemed suddenly released from an unbearable tension and she sagged against his length, burying her head in his chest again, murmuring incoherently against his shirt-front.

'Hey,' he protested, 'I can't understand a word you're saying down there! Besides which,' he raised her chin again with his forefinger, 'I want your face up here.' The finger went from chin to each cheek in turn, wiping away the tears that had spilled over.

His eyes lifted then to the luminous glow in hers, and she saw their darkening as his head bent and his lips touched the soft outline of her mouth.

It was as if they had never kissed before, never known a kiss as a prelude to the easily kindled passion between them. Jay's mouth moved slowly, almost tentatively, over hers, and her response was a wondering acceptance of a shiny new relationship.

Jay's breath came only a little faster when he finally raised his head and said unsteadily: 'Let's take it in easy stages.' He looked across the room. 'And I think the first stage should take place on that sofa over there.'

Although the distance was short, he swung her up in his arms and carried her there, depositing her with her head comfortably raised on a cushion.

He didn't lie down beside her; instead, he sat at

an angle facing her, his thigh taut and warm against hers. 'There's a couple of things I want to tell you before we proceed to stage two. Things I missed out the other day.'

'You told me about buying the *Queen*, and getting the—contract,' she wrinkled her brow in question. 'Can there be more?'

'There can,' he stated gravely, and picked up her hand to twine his own fingers through hers. 'I made a condition when I made the ship deal with Jacob.'

'Condition?' she queried.

'I'm not so sure it's a good one now, but it seemed a good idea at the time.'

'Jay, for heaven's sake tell me before I die of curiosity!'

'Well,' he said slowly, 'I insisted that my wife was to be fully responsible for the ship.'

'Me?' she interjected, her eyes widening to saucers. 'But how can I keep on sailing in her when we live in Chicago?'

'I didn't say anything about you sailing in her,' he corrected, his free hand moving disturbingly up from her thigh over the sharp rise of her breast to stroke gently, almost absently, the soft skin of her throat. 'I said you were to be responsible for her, work with the designers on the interior layout, then choose colours and so on.'

'It's still a long way from Chicago,' she doubted, her enthusiasm dampened. Doing all the things Jay had suggested would be exciting, fulfilling, but not something a person could do from thousands of miles away.

'I know Chicago is a long way away,' he returned

patiently, 'but you won't be. Didn't I tell you I'm opening up a new office tower in L.A.?'

Toni shot up straight, almost dislodging him from the sofa's edge. 'You're doing *what*?'

'I said I'm——'

'I heard you,' she interrupted impatiently. 'Does that mean that—we'll be living at the Coast?'

'I thought you might like the idea. There are some nice places around where Jacob and his family live. Sea views, clean air, lots of room for kids to roam around. And dogs. I've always wanted to have dogs.'

'I can't believe it.' Toni's mind was working overtime with all the ramifications of such a move. 'What about staff? Would you—transfer everybody from Chicago?'

'Some, but most of them will stay right there. I thought we could keep the apartment there for when we pay our flying visits.' He gave an unexpected chuckle. 'If you're wondering about Gloria you don't have to. Unless I'm way off base, I think she's transferred her interest to Cyrus.'

'Seriously?' Toni was thoughtful for a moment. 'I like Cyrus. I wouldn't want to see him hurt.'

'He can take care of himself,' Jay assured her, a wry smile stretching his lips, '*and* Gloria. I think she might have bitten off more than she can chew this time.' He pushed Toni gently back into her former position, and this time he arranged his lean length beside her. Toni slid her arms up over his chest to his shoulders, loving the familiar feel, the familiar smell, of him.

'I love you, Jay Stanford.'

'And I love you, Antonia.'

A long time later Toni stirred and murmured huskily: 'How many—dogs?'

'One—for—each—child,' he muttered against her lips, and blotted away her smile with his kiss.

Here's how to get your volume NOW!

MAIL IN	$	GET
2 SPECIAL PROOF-OF-PURCHASE SEALS*	PLUS $1 U.S.	ONE BOOK
5 SPECIAL PROOF-OF-PURCHASE SEALS*	PLUS 50¢ U.S.	ONE BOOK
8 SPECIAL PROOF-OF-PURCHASE SEALS*	FREE	ONE BOOK

*Special proof-of-purchase seal from inside back cover of all specially marked Harlequin "Let Your Imagination Fly Sweepstakes" volumes. No other proof-of-purchase accepted.

ORDERING DETAILS:

Print your name, address, city, state or province, zip or postal code on the coupon below or a plain 3" x 5" piece of paper and together with the special proof-of-purchase seals and check or money order (no stamps or cash please) as indicated. Mail to:

HARLEQUIN ROMANCE TREASURY BOOK OFFER P.O. BOX 1399 MEDFORD, N.Y. 11763, U.S.A.

Make check or money order payable to: Harlequin Romance Treasury Offer. Allow 3 to 4 weeks for delivery.

Special offer expires: June 30, 1981

PLEASE PRINT

Name

Address

Apt. No.

City

State/ Prov.

Zip/Postal Code

Let Your Imagination Fly Sweepstakes

Rules and Regulations:

NO PURCHASE NECESSARY

1   Enter the Let Your Imagination Fly Sweepstakes 1, 2 or 3 as often as you wish. Mail each entry form separately bearing sufficient postage Specify the sweepstake you wish to enter on the outside of the envelope Mail a completed entry form or, your name, address, and telephone number printed on a plain 3"x 5" piece of paper to:

HARLEQUIN LET YOUR IMAGINATION FLY SWEEPSTAKES,

P O BOX 1280, MEDFORD, N Y 11763 U.S.A.

2   Each completed entry form must be accompanied by I Let Your Imagination Fly proof-of-purchase seal from the back inside cover of specially marked Let Your Imagination Fly Harlequin books (or the words "Let Your Imagination Fly" printed on a plain 3"x 5" piece of paper Specify by number the Sweepstakes you are entering on the outside of the envelope

3   The prize structure for each sweepstake is as follows:

Sweepstake 1 - North America

Grand Prize winner's choice: a one-week trip for two to either Bermuda; Montreal, Canada; or San Francisco. 3 Grand Prizes will be awarded (min approx retail value $1,375 U S., based on Chicago departure) and 4,000 First Prizes: scarves by nik nik, worth $14 U S each. All prizes will be awarded

Sweepstake 3 - Caribbean

Grand Prize winner's choice: a one-week trip for two to either Nassau, Bahamas; San Juan, Puerto Rico; or St Thomas, Virgin Islands. 3 Grand Prizes will be awarded. (Min. approx. retail value $1,650 U.S., based on Chicago departure) and 4,000 First Prizes: simulated diamond pendants by Kenneth Jay Lane, worth $15 U.S. each. All prizes will be awarded.

Sweepstake 3 - Europe

Grand Prize winner's choice: a one-week trip for two to either London, England; Frankfurt, Germany; Paris, France; or Rome, Italy 3 Grand Prizes will be awarded. (Min. approx retail value $2,800 U S., based on Chicago departure) and 4,000 First Prizes: 1/2 oz. bottles of perfume, BLAZER by Anne Klein (Retail value over $30 U S) All prizes will be awarded.

Grand trip prizes will include coach round-trip airfare for two persons from the nearest commercial airport serviced by Delta Air Lines to the city as designated in the prize, double occupancy accommodation at a first-class or medium hotel, depending on vacation, and $500 U.S. spending money Departure taxes, visas, passports, ground transportation to and from airports will be the responsibility of the winners.

4   To be eligible, Sweepstakes entries must be received as follows:

Sweepstake 1 Entries received by February 28, 1981
Sweepstake 2 Entries received by April 30, 1981
Sweepstake 3 Entries received by June 30, 1981
Make sure you enter each Sweepstake separately since entries will not be carried forward from one Sweepstake to the next.

The odds of winning will be determined by the number of entries received in each of the three sweepstakes. Canadian residents, in order to win any prize, will be required to first correctly answer a time-limited skill-testing question, to be posed by telephone, at a mutually convenient time

5   Random selections to determine Sweepstake 1, 2 or 3 winners will be conducted by Lee Krost Associates, an independent judging organization whose decisions are final. Only one prize per family, per sweepstake Prizes are non-transferable and non-refundable and no substitutions will be allowed. Winners will be responsible for any applicable federal, state and local taxes. Trips must be taken during normal tour periods before June 30, 1982 Reservations will be on a space-available basis. Airline tickets are non-transferable, non-refundable and non-redeemable for cash

6   The Let Your Imagination Fly Sweepstakes is open to all residents of the United States of America and Canada, (excluding the Province of Quebec) except employees and their immediate families of Harlequin Enterprises Ltd., its advertising agencies, Marketing & Promotion Group Canada Ltd and Lee Krost Associates, Inc , the independent judging company Winners may be required to furnish proof of eligibility Void wherever prohibited or restricted by law All federal, state, provincial and local laws apply

7   For a list of trip winners, send a stamped, self-addressed envelope to:

Harlequin Trip Winners List, P O Box 1401, MEDFORD, N Y 11763 U S A.

Winners lists will be available after the last sweepstake has been conducted and winners determined. NO PURCHASE NECESSARY

Let Your Imagination Fly Sweepstakes

OFFICIAL ENTRY FORM

Please enter me in Sweepstake No. _____

Please print:

Name

Address

Apt No.   City

State/   Zip/Postal
Prov   Code

Telephone No.   area code
(   )

MAIL TO:
HARLEQUIN LET YOUR
IMAGINATION FLY SWEEPSTAKE No._____
P.O. BOX 1280,
MEDFORD, N.Y. 11763 U.S.A.

(Please specify by number, the Sweepstake you are entering.)